RANDY COATES

More Precious than Rubies

The Return of the Norse Gods

iUniverse, Inc.
Bloomington

More Precious than Rubies
The Return of the Norse Gods

iUniverse books may be ordered through booksellers or by contacting:

iUniverse
1663 Liberty Drive
Bloomington, IN 47403
www.iuniverse.com
1-800-Authors (1-800-288-4677)

Because of the dynamic nature of the Internet, any web addresses or links contained in this book may have changed since publication and may no longer be valid. The views expressed in this work are solely those of the author and do not necessarily reflect the views of the publisher, and the publisher hereby disclaims any responsibility for them.

Any people depicted in stock imagery provided by Thinkstock are models, and such images are being used for illustrative purposes only.

Certain stock imagery © Thinkstock.

ISBN: 978-1-4759-2660-6 (sc)
ISBN: 978-1-4759-2662-0 (e)
ISBN: 978-1-4759-2661-3 (dj)

Library of Congress Control Number: 2012909149

Printed in the United States of America

iUniverse rev. date: 5/24/2012

Table of Contents

Part 1

Chapter 1: The Tale of Iduna's Apples

Paul Brager, twelve-years-old, knew that his father's presence in his bedroom at this hour could only mean one thing. He was there for his nightly ritual, the telling of the bedtime story for Paul's younger brother, Adrian.

Paul had claimed the top bunk of the bunk bed for himself long ago, allowing Adrian no choice but to sleep in the lower bunk. That's what big brothers did, Paul thought. They asserted power over their younger brothers. They got to pick what was on television and they got to use the computer first and they got to confiscate whatever bunk they wanted before their brother had a chance.

Mr. Brager settled himself in a chair across from the lower bed where Adrian was lying. "Once long ago...," he began.

"Once upon a time."

"Huh?"

"All stories start 'Once upon a time.' You always start them with 'Once upon a time.'"

"Well I was just trying to be a little different. A little spontaneous."

"A little...spon-what-eous?"

Mr. Brager looked at the crooked grin of his youngest son and appeared to be amused. This had always been a game: to chuck in a word that was more complicated than the rest and to get Adrian asking questions. Wasn't that the point of childhood? Brager always said to his sons – to keep kids curious and to make them see that questions were more important than answers.

Adrian pulled his bedsheets up to his chin, waiting, although the June air was sultry, sneaking through the bedroom's open window, rolling over and around the room lazily.

Adrian still had goosebumps. Every night he did, anticipating his father's story. Knowing it would somehow lull him to sleep and make him forget about the death of his mother.

"Spon-tay-knee-us," Brager said slowly.

"Spon-tay-me-us."

"Knee-us."

"Knee-us."

"Knee-us, knee-us, knee-us," grumbled Paul, turning angrily on his bed.

"Now, now," Mr. Brager said sternly.

Adrian didn't seem to notice this interruption. "What's it mean, Dad?"

"What? Oh...Spontaneous means to do something without really thinking about it...To do it suddenly."

Adrian screwed up his face but it was more for dramatics than anything. "But...that's bad, isn't it?"

"Sometimes. But not this time."

"Why...?"

"Jeeeezzz...Let him get on with the story." It was bad enough that Paul had to share a room with his eight-year-old brother but that he also had to be subjected to the nightly story-telling. Some nights, he even took his sleeping bag outside when the weather was fine and set up the tent in the backyard just to avoid the routine.

"Okay Dad. On with the story before Paul takes a snit fit."

Paul put his pillow over his head.

"Once...upon a time..."

Adrian put his blanket down and settled himself.

"...there was a woman called Iduna..." He could see that Adrian was about to raise himself up and to inquire about this unusual name, but his finger raised to his lips made Adrian keep still. "...Iduna happened to be a goddess who had very special powers. But her powers were also very simple. In fact, her powers came in the form of apples..."

Again, his finger went to his lips.

"Iduna had a whole orchard of apples but these were not your ordinary apples. They were the most delicious apples that you ever tasted and once you tasted them..."

Adrian's eyes were wide.

Paul stirred. The pillow came off of his head and he turned over onto his back, staring at the ceiling.

"...Once you tasted them," Brager continued, moving back so that he now had a good view of both of his sons, "you felt different. You felt younger and stronger and full of energy. And as long as you kept eating them, you would never age. Never get older than what your age was now."

"Coool."

"Iduna used to let the gods come into the orchard and eat the apples. It made them strong for battle. But there was also a problem."

Adrian propped himself up on one elbow.

"Bad people wanted the apples, too. You see, that's the thing about special items. People get greedy. Sometimes, they'll steal for them. Sometimes, they'll even kill for them." Here, Brager checked the reaction of Adrian as if he were registering any change in his son's expression. Adrian's erratic nod allowed him to continue. "So Iduna had to watch over the apples. To make sure no bad people got at them. But she was tricked into leaving her orchard."

"How?"

"Even though Loki was one of the gods, he had a bad attitude..." Paul snickered at this. "He was a trickster. He approached Iduna and told her that he had seen other apples that were much better than hers. Tastier. Redder. More powerful. You see, his intention was to take Iduna away from the orchard, to show her these other apples. Even though her husband pleaded with her not to go, her pride was hurt. She couldn't ignore her curiosity..."

"So she went?"

"I'm afraid she did."

Paul turned on his side to watch his father. There was something about his father's storytelling tonight that seemed to be troubling Mr. Brager.

"Not long after Loki and Iduna left, there was a terrible thumping in the sky above them. Like the beating of a thousand wings. Iduna looked up and saw this massive eagle coming at her. Iduna had no time to react. Before she knew it, the bird grabbed her in its talons and swept her into the air. It flew off."

"Well...Who was it? I mean, I know it was an eagle but..."

"It was really a giant in the form of an eagle. The giants were the enemies of the gods and this one had wanted the whole orchard for himself. It had captured Loki and said it would give Loki his freedom back only if he tricked Iduna into leaving the apples."

"So what happened to...I...Idoo...?"

"That's another story which I'll tell you another day...So then, because Iduna was missing, bad things happened. In her absence, the land began to shrivel and die. Leaves fell from trees, things turned brown. But, worst of all, the gods started to get old because they no longer had Iduna around to provide them with the apples." Brager stopped then and closed his eyes.

After a long pause, Adrian said, "Is that it? That's the end?"

"You know my stories never end, son. There is always a continuation. Just like in life. One story begins where another has ended."

"Just like in a T.V. show."

"Exactly."

"But..."

"Yes?"

"There is no happy ending. I think it should have a happy ending. I mean...I'm not dumb...I know there are sad endings, too, but..."

"There is a happy ending, Adrian."

Paul kicked his feet over the side of the bed and started down the ladder.

Brager moved back to let him pass. "Are you okay, Paul?"

"Sure I'm okay. Why shouldn't I be?"

"I was almost finished."

"I just wanted to get a drink. It's pretty hot."

After Paul was out of the room, Adrian asked, "Do the gods get better? Does...I-doo-na...return? Does the giant die?"

Brager said nothing for awhile.

Paul appeared in the doorway, a can of coca-cola in his grip. From where he stood, he thought he could see his dad's eyes moistening.

"Dad?"

Mr. Brager opened his eyes and wiped them with one hand. "There's a happy ending, Adrian. This one has a happy ending. Don't worry. The giant gets it in the end."

"Good!" Adrian clapped his hands together. "Are you okay?"

Brager brushed the bangs out of his son's eyes. "Yeah, I'm okay."

Adrian smiled one of those comforting smiles that only children can deliver, those smiles that are confident and have yet to be damaged by time. "You haven't told me that story before."

"No, I haven't."

"That's kind of weird."

"Why's that?"

"You usually run out of stories and tell me one I've heard before...Don't get me wrong, Dad...I like them."

"I know, I know...I guess it just seemed like the right time...To tell that story, I mean."

Paul walked back out to the kitchen.

Mr. Brager stood up, then knelt down as quickly as he had gotten up. "Oh man."

"What?"

"I forgot the most important part of the story."

"So there is more! Should we get Paul?"

"No, no, that's okay. I think he's outgrowing the stories, anyway...When the gods saw what the stealing of Iduna's apples caused in the land – all the heartbreak it caused – they decided to do something about it. They decided to hide all the apples..."

"The whole orchard?"

"The whole orchard..."

"No way!"

"...They did this because they now knew what evil people could do with them. That's the problem in the world, you see. When good things are put in the hands of the wrong people...then bad things happen. So the gods hid them. And to this day, the apples remain hidden. No one knows where they are."

Adrian said nothing for a very long time, then finally, "They're hidden in *our* world?"

"Could be."

"Dad, where'd ya hear this?"

Brager smiled. "It's actually a myth. You know what...?"

"Yeah, yeah...It's not real...You have a good memory."

"I made up a little bit of it. That's what a good story-teller does...Each time he retells a story, he does it a little bit different. So he doesn't bore the audience. But, most of all, so he doesn't bore himself...Hey, I'm gonna let you sleep now."

"Yeah, you'd better get Paul or he's gonna drink all the coke."

Brager found Paul sitting at the kitchen table, the empty coke can in front of him. He sat down beside him.

"Yeah, I'm okay, Dad."

"Fine, fine."

"I get it, you know."

"Get what?"

"The story. Iduna is really Ida, isn't she?"

Ida was Brager's wife, killed in a car accident five years ago when Paul was seven and Adrian was only three.

Paul swallowed with difficulty. The death of his mother had affected him greatly when it happened. There had been a drunk driver (or at least people insisted he was drunk) who had rammed into his parents' car when they were coming back from visiting friends.

Luckily, Paul and Adrian were at home with a babysitter and not involved in the accident.

Mr. Brager had been injured slightly but was emotionally devastated about his wife's death.

Paul remembered that his father had said very little to him and Adrian about the tragedy, as if he didn't want to upset them. Paul gained most of the information concerning the accident from other people. He also recalled seeing a grainy image of the *drunk* driver in the newspaper. Ironically, his dad worked as a writer for that very newspaper.

Brager grinned. "I figured you would get that part. About Iduna, I mean." He put his hand out to stroke his son's cheek but Paul turned his head to avoid the touch.

"What d'ya mean, *that part*? I got all of it."

"Oh really?"

"Yeah, really."

"So what do you think the apples signify?" he asked, unsettled. There was something in the way he asked the question that made him look as if he wasn't sure of the answer himself.

Paul showed defiance. "They're the things in life we can't get, right? The good things we wish for that we can never have. Like, nobody lives forever...Like thinking you'll always have a mother and then finding out..."

This time, Paul did not flinch when Brager reached out and touched his shoulder.

"Sometimes, things turn out okay. Not always, but sometimes."

"I don't know, Dad. Maybe you shouldn't be telling stories like that."

"Why?"

"Well...I don't know."

"Did you like them when you were younger?"

Paul cracked a half-hearted grin. "Yeah, I guess I did."

"Paul, in some stories, bad things happen. As you know, in life, bad things happen. I believe that bad things remind us to be hopeful."

"For the good things?"

"Yeah. Now you'd better go to bed. You've got a whole summer stretched out ahead of you."

Chapter 2: The Stranger

The first long weekend of the summer had arrived and Paul was feeling a lot better than he was the other night, the night his dad made him think about his mom again. His dad really meant well, Paul knew, he just seemed to be pleasing himself too much with those wild tales.

In fact, Paul was feeling pretty good just now. School had let out, he believed that Liz Parkinson liked him, and he'd be going into grade seven come September. He and his classmates, so Paul was thinking, would be pretty much kings at Dorian Heights.

Everything was sweet. Right now, anyway.

There was the whole summer ahead and he had no commitments except for that part-time job thing that Chad Tremblay, his best friend, and he had about cutting lawns in their neighbourhood. Yeah, he'd actually be making some money. And though Chad had more of the entrepreneurial spirit than Paul – he was the one who had secured the jobs for them in the first place – Paul wasn't going to turn down his first money-making opportunity. Mr. Tremblay told them in his joking (though it was hard to tell with him) way that they were *materialistic*. Then he lit up a cigarette and said out of the side of his mouth, like he was trying to impersonate a gangster and not doing very well at it, "I suppose you kids gotta start makin' money some time. Tough world."

Paul could sense the sun through his short-sleeved Raptors shirt. His arms were already beginning to be barbecued brown. He was well aware of ozone depletion and global warming and that basking too much in the sun would roast his innards and cause cancer. The teachers had taught the subject to death in the weather and conservation of energy units in science. But he was in such a great mood, school already distant in his thoughts, that he refused to focus on the effects of the sun. People usually die before the sun gets to them, he thought, his mother's face swimming up into his mind. Then, he told himself to shut up.

"Hey Paul!"

The sound came to his right and there was Tremblay, standing by the swan boats, pointing at them with a delicious grin and motioning him over.

He approached in disbelief. "Are you kidding?" Only one boat was in use, occupied by a woman, probably a grandmother, and a tiny, black-haired girl who looked to be four or five. The woman could not hide her boredom but the kid was loving it, throwing her head back and letting out loud, annoying bursts of laughter.

"Let's go for it."

Chad had inherited his sense of humour from his dad. Paul could never tell when he was joking and he had to be careful because, too often, he ended up putting Chad in a mood when he questioned the validity of his comments.

But, come on, he thought, this had to be a joke. "But this is so..." He double-checked Chad's face and caught the tell-tale smirk. "But it's so..." He stopped before he said something offensive.

The students at Dorian Heights knew well enough that some words were taboo. For instance, they were pretty good at intervening when their friends got too close to being racist. But, as teachers kept reminding them, they now had to work on not using other words that bordered on insult.

He didn't need to say anything more. Chad laughed a laugh that challenged the girl's. Her grandmother twisted around in the boat, looking ridiculous with the swan wings coming up around her, and almost fell into the water.

That got both Paul and Chad going.

The grandmother made a shrewd face and said something unpleasant to the girl whose face was screwed up in obvious ignorance. She clapped her French fry fingers to her round, little face and joined Paul and Chad in their happiness.

Paul and Chad loped off, the shrill laughter chasing them into other parts of Centre Island.

"Oh don't...Oh don't..." Chad stuttered through the machine gun fire of laughs. "Oh, don't...do that!...Be kind to your...el...Your el...Your el-derrrrrsss!"

"Now," Paul croaked, taking on the voice of an old man, "you think this is funny now..."

His old man voice always killed Chad. Chad couldn't even look at him. He bent his head down over his forearm and shuddered as Paul went on.

"Just wait until yer my age, kiddo. Then you'll know... You'll know how it feels...Life's not all fun and games. You'll see."

They flopped onto a clean piece of grass, making sure there were no goose droppings to land in, and watched the odd stares of people passing, their eyes twinkling.

When Chad eventually reclaimed his voice, he grinned hugely at Paul and nudged him with the toe of his running shoe. "You would've got in if Parkinson had invited you."

Paul didn't know what he was talking about at first, then understood. He shook his head, wondering how Chad knew about him and Liz.

"Yeah, right, Brager. A little kiss, kiss, smooch, smooch with Parkinson in your own personal swan boat."

"Oh shut up!" He wanted to say something else but every time he swore, the words didn't taste good in his mouth. As if his body were rejecting them, letting him get older.

"Everyone knows!"

He could've played dumb and said *Knows what?* but that wasn't the way Chad and he worked. They knew each other too well to pretend or treat the other like an idiot. Paul stared at him, slightly defiant. "Okay, but does she like me?"

"Come on, you know she does."

Even though Paul was probably aware of Liz's feelings towards him, he felt a surge of warmth (and it sure wasn't the sun) slide right up and down in the middle of him. He was convinced that Chad could see it, radiating right out of him and, for that, he grew embarrassed. He hated giving in to the lovey-dovey feeling. He had to make himself think about action movies in order to get rid of it. He also needed to turn the subject back around and hit Chad with it.

"What about you and..." He tried to picture the other girls in their grade six class, their faces already disappearing from memory. "...Sylvia?" It was what he thought an outrageous choice. Chad usually kept to himself when it came to girls and Paul really didn't know if he were attracted to any of them in their class. He chose Sylvia out of the blue. She was kind of cute but a little withdrawn and delicate. She never said much.

Without any hesitation or surprise that Paul had stumbled onto the right choice, Chad said, "Do you think she likes me?"

Paul almost bellowed laughter over his gamble, but looked away so he could bring on a magical transformation of expression. "Yeah, I think she does." Frankly, he had never even seen the two share a conversation, let alone a look.

Chad must have mistaken his confusion for something else because he said, "You think she's ugly, don't you?"

"No, no. I think she's cute." That was all Chad needed to hear.

They sat quietly for a few minutes, watching tired families pass by.

"Where did your dad say he'd meet us?"

"Uh...by the ferry dock...I think he said around three." Chad cupped his hands around his eyes to block out the sun and glanced over at Wesley's Restaurant in the distance.

"It's almost three."

"Yeah, well, you gotta understand something about my dad..." *My dad.* Chad never referred to him simply as *Dad.* "His three is usually three-thirty." He looked over at Wesley's again. "Especially when there's a place nearby where he can have a beer and a smoke."

Paul followed his gaze and nodded, thinking quickly of how to change the subject. "So we hang out a little longer?"

"I'd say so...but I gotta take a pee." He got up and left for the washroom.

Paul lay back on the grass, waiting for his return, but a strange sensation came over him, something mysterious that urged him to jar himself up and look ahead.

There appeared nothing unusual at first: just a middle-aged man reclining beneath a tree. Paul looked around for anything that might seem out-of-place, anything that the sensation was forcing him to discover. He almost lay back again, making fun of himself for being silly and superstitious, when he took a second look at the man.

He looked to be about his dad's age, perhaps late-thirties, early forties. His full head of hair had not been touched by grey yet – at the sides, just above the ears where his father's hair was turning grey. Three things about the man struck Paul as weird.

First, he was wearing a dark suit. He had taken the jacket off but his tie was still pinned there, making the man's neck look scrunched-up. Not that wearing a suit was a big deal to Paul. In church, it was natural. But here on Centre Island? Among the goose deposits and the suffocating heat? That just wasn't right. But despite this, the man looked totally unaffected by the environment.

Secondly, the man was chewing, almost laboriously, on an apple. At least eating an apple seemed more realistic to Paul than the suit-thing; however, it was the way he was eating it. Almost as if there was a mine hidden away in it and he had to be careful about chomping down.

But the third thing that really made Paul uncomfortable was that the man was staring straight at him and smiling. When he casually flicked away his apple core and took another from his bag nearby, Paul remembered the story his father had told the other night, the one about Iduna's apples.

"What's with you?"

Chad's words startled him. "Don't do that."

"Why you looking so weird? What'd I miss?"

"Check out that guy."

Chad rolled his eyes. "What now, Brager?"

"I don't know. Don't look too fast. He's still looking... Wait. He just looked away."

The man got up into a sitting position, his back against the tree. He seemed to be interested in something on the far side of the park. For the first time, Paul noticed how truly tall and well-built the man was. It seemed strange to him how even the suit could accentuate his muscles.

Chad took a look. "What are you worried about?"

"Well, before you came, he was looking at me and smiling."

"Maybe he thinks you're funny." Chad sighed. "You're always making things up, Brager. Last time, you thought that lady was some kind of spy." Chad took another look at the man.

Paul kicked Chad's foot harder than he wanted to. "Maybe he's a retard."

The teachers had cautioned them about using that word too but Paul let it go.

The man turned around and looked at them. "You guys have the time?" He must have finished the second apple because he had nothing in his hand. He slowly stood up, taking care not to hit his head on a branch, and brushed himself off.

Paul and Chad were frozen.

The man picked up his bag, blue with vibrant, yellow lettering on it. "The time?" he said, tapping his wrist. "Watch is broken."

"Uh...Jeez, it's three-fifteen, Chad. We should go and meet your dad now." Paul said this last line overly loud but his voice sounded squeaky.

"Three-fifteen. Thanks." The man approached them and they could see a big black ring on his left hand, glinting in the sun. The man looked down at his hand. "It's bloodstone. That's what it's called."

Paul and Chad said nothing but slowly got to their feet. "Uh, seeya!"

"Hey," he said and they turned. "Just to let you know, I'm a teacher. A principal, in fact." He held up his bag and it had the letters E-T-F-O on it. Paul and Chad had seen teachers in their school with the same bag. "Stands for *Elementary Teachers' Federation of Ontario.*"

They nodded and started to walk away.

"Have a good day!"

"You too, spy," Chad said quietly and this got them laughing again. Then they broke into a run, convincing themselves that their speed had more to do with their lateness than with wanting to get out of there.

Mr. Tremblay looked upset when they met him but he said nothing except, "Let's go."

"Hey...uh..."

Tremblay turned to look at Chad. "What?"

"We think we just saw a...Well, there was this guy."

"What?"

"Well," Paul said, jumping in because Chad was now looking timid, "we're not sure he was ...strange. You know? Strange in any way."

Tremblay stood still, watching them, his hands on his hips. "Now come on, either he's a weirdo or he isn't. What did he do?"

"He just talked to us. I mean...He asked us for the time."

"Did he say anything...you know...*nuts* to you?"

This was Tremblay's conclusion about any person who was out-of-the-ordinary to him. The person was *nuts* or *a nutso*.

Tremblay approached them and they could see that his face had a fresh pink colour but they weren't sure if it had got that way from sun or beer.

"I'm sorry we're late," Paul said, trying to evade the subject. After all, the guy probably really was a principal.

One that overstepped his boundaries nonetheless. He purposely left Chad out of the apology, hoping Tremblay would not give Chad a hard time when they got home. Tremblay had a tendency to over-react.

"Did he...do...anything?"

Now Tremblay was so close that they could smell the beer.

Both boys shook their head, neither willing to volunteer any more information.

"Well where is he?"

And that was exactly the difference between Mr. Brager and Mr. Tremblay. Brager would have dismissed the subject at this point. Tremblay would still want a confrontation even though he had no truth to go on.

"I shouldn't have said anything," Chad turned to Paul but he said it loud enough so his father could hear.

"Now wait, wait," said Tremblay, "if this guy's a weirdo, we have to tell the police. There are a lot of kids around."

"Mr. Tremblay," Paul said, almost pleadingly, "he really didn't do anything to us. He just talked...but not weird stuff...I mean, he didn't ask for our phone number or anything personal..."

Tremblay stood back, looking at them. Then he stared at Chad and shook his head. "You're right. You shouldn't have said anything." Then he swung around and continued walking but it was an angry walk.

When the ferry came, Paul and Chad distanced themselves from Mr. Tremblay. Chad looked out over Toronto Harbour and Paul could tell from the tight skin around his jaw that Chad was clenching his teeth and trying not to cry.

"Hey Chad..."

"I hate him, I hate him, I hate him." Then the tears came bubbling at the corners of his eyes.

"Chad..."

"I knew I shouldn't have told him about it." Paul wanted to ask why he did but he got the answer anyway. "But he's got this way...Sometimes, you know, I feel I have to tell him...As if he'll find out about it anyway even when I don't..."

"Okay, I get it."

Chad wiped his eyes. "I wish I had a father like yours... He's so good."

They stood and watched the gulls circling on the water and then Paul said, "That guy was a little weird though. I really don't think he was a, you know, criminal."

"But even teachers don't talk to kids who don't belong to their own school."

"Exactly."

"Didja see how tall he was, man?"

"Yeah, yeah." Paul could see that Chad was getting back to his old self and showing more animation.

They were quiet for the rest of the journey back to the mainland.

However, there was something still bothering Paul.

Something about that man.

Paul knew, without a doubt, he had seen him before. But where?

Chapter 3: The Arrival of the New Principal

Chad and Paul, despite seeing each other almost every day throughout the summer, still managed a high-five in the school's foyer when school started again in September. As if they hadn't seen each other in years. Mrs. Dexter kindly reminded them that it was a beautiful day and that they could take their celebratory moods outside.

As they walked their way to an exit, a tall man walked confidently into the building. They identified him immediately as he stopped before them and tipped his head. He wore a suit very similar to the one he was wearing when they first met him but a briefcase was there to replace his ETFO bag.

"Well, well, well," he said smugly and when the two boys remained mute, he said, "I wouldn't call this a coincidence, boys. No, not at all. In fact, I had a strong feeling we'd meet again. That's why I was so friendly on the island. I could sense your discomfort then but I couldn't succeed in dispelling it."

Paul didn't like the way he said *dispelling*, the word coming out greasy and threatening. At least when his dad introduced new vocabulary, he never sounded as if he were lecturing to his sons.

"Are you...?" Chad started. "Are you actually...stalking us?"

The man doubled over, his roar of laughter bouncing off the school walls. "Oh, good God, no! Oh, that's funny."

Paul poked Chad on the shoulder. "I think he's going to be teaching here, dude. Welcome, sir." Paul put out his hand.

"Well, thank you. My name is Theisen. Mr. Theisen." When he shook Paul's hand, Paul almost groaned in pain, but he held on to the grip and never let an expression cross his face.

"Paul. I'm Paul. This is my friend, Chad."

Chad held out his hand reluctantly and steadied himself for the attack. "You're pretty strong, Mr..."

"Theisen," he said one more time. He picked up his briefcase which he had put against the wall, then held up his wrist. "Watch is all fixed now. Can't be without time, you know. Reminds us that we're getting older."

"Well, Mr...Theisen. We gotta be outside. School rules, you know."

"Take care."

The boys scurried outside and were almost bowled over by Michael Simmons, who had grown taller over the summer.

Funny. Back in grade three, when they had first met him, they used to look at Michael with admiration, considering him the tallest kid in grade three classes all over the world. They and the other students claimed him as their hero, the subject of fame. That was until they really got to know him.

Michael immediately picked up from when they had seen him in June. As if he'd been on pause all summer and someone had just pushed the *play* button. There he was spluttering something about Mr. Myers, their principal. Something tragic, the way Michael was telling it. By the time they got Michael calmed down, they learned it wasn't so much a tragedy at all.

"What are you saying, Michael? Remember, slowly."

"He's gone. He won't be back. Everyone's surprised, even the teachers. There was no warning. You know how I know all this? My mom's on the Parent Council..."

That is, Mrs. Simmons was on the Parent Council the year before. The Council this year wasn't even formed yet. Michael liked to exaggerate things.

"So maybe something really bad happened. Maybe Mr. Myers died."

Michael shook his head wildly. "Unh-uh. Mom and I saw him last month at the grocery store." It was just like Michael to pinpoint every detail. "Mom asked him if he was ready for school and he just kinda looked down and said nothin'. Looked real sad. Mom asked him what was wrong and he said 'I won't be back at Dorian Heights.' Just like that. 'I won't be back at Dorian Heights.' Didn't even look at us when he said it. Mom asked why and he said he had been transferred. Mom asked why again and he said he couldn't discuss it..."

"Maybe he did something really bad here."

The female voice startled them. The three of them had been so involved in the discussion that they hadn't noticed the small crowd that had formed behind them. At the front of it was Liz Parkinson. When Paul turned, she smiled mischievously at him and he felt stupid and blushed.

As Paul took in the scene around him, he noticed how the schoolyard had filled up. Kids wore fresh, new clothes just waiting to be soiled, and hoisted sparkling knapsacks.

They were being watched by amused parents and being greeted by overly-friendly teachers wearing nametags.

"Mr. Myers was a nice guy," another voice said. "I can't imagine him doing anythin' wrong...Besides, some teachers get transferred for good reasons."

"Like what?"

"Like helping a school that's fallin' apart. My friend's dad was a principal. That's why he got transferred."

"What d'ya mean a school that's *fallin' apart?*"

"You know, one that's really bad. One where the kids are taking over."

"Like ours," someone giggled.

"Worse."

"Where there are fights everyday," said Liz. Everyone decided to stop talking and nodded. Liz always had this voice of reason, one that even the older kids stopped to listen to.

"Anyway," Michael said, "he seemed real sad in the store. Who knows why he got transferred. Whatever, he sure wasn't happy about it."

"Did he say the name of the school?"

Michael shook his head.

"He seemed okay back in June. He was in a real good mood. I gave him some chocolates and he said he'd see me in September."

"So he must've found out about the transfer in July or August. That's not really fair."

"And have you met the new principal?"

This new voice came rumbling from somewhere in the back of the growing mob. They recognized the assertive, all-knowing voice of Arif Khaled. Whereas Michael Simmons loved to deliver news and gossip at a breakneck speed, Arif was always stretching it out so painfully that everyone was in suspense. He got quite a bit of attention this way and he knew it.

They waited, knowing his style.

"He was out just ten minutes ago, introducing himself to the kids and parents. You gotta keep on top of these things, guys."

Paul and Chad eyed each other, knowing exactly what the other was thinking.

"He's kind of eerie. Like he wants to eat you right after he stops smiling at you."

Paul remembered that day on Centre Island, the first time the smile had been revealed to him.

Arif was envied because he always got to see the R-rated horror movies before the rest of them did. His parents owned a movie theatre and Arif's older brother was always sneaking him in for free. Arif always had crowds around him because he was good at describing every bloody detail in the latest monster movie. He was always promising he'd get all of them in for free but never went any further than that.

"He's real scary-looking."

"What d'ya mean by that?"

Paul glanced at Chad and could see a range of emotions on his face. He could tell that Chad was aching to jump in, to outdo Arif and tell everyone that he and Paul had met Theisen long before Arif had ever heard about him. But Paul knew he wouldn't say a word because it brought back memories of his dad, memories he probably wished he could delete.

Arif produced a huge grin. "Well, he's dressed in a suit and tie. He has this lah-dee-dah look goin' on but... He's just...It's like there's something under his skin, ready to break out."

There were hoots of amusement. A few kids slapped Arif's arm playfully. They were familiar with his technique: trying to make reality resemble something from one of his movies.

"You mean his skin will melt off, Arif?"

"Yeah, and underneath the melted skin, we'll see computer chips."

A few choice swear words were directed at Arif while some of the more self-conscious kids shushed the others, reminding them that teachers lurked nearby.

"Was he the guy in the blue suit and red tie?" Liz asked.

Arif nodded.

"He *is* kind of creepy-looking."

There were some more hoots.

Chad turned around to face Michael. "What about Mrs. Tarnapulsky? Is she back?"

Mrs. Tarnapulsky was the vice-principal.

"Jeez, I don't know. Wouldn't it be weird...?"

"She's back," someone interjected. "I saw her in the office."

The bell rang, that old, irritating sound that had been thankfully absent from their lives in the last two months. There was a flurry of activity as parents said goodbye to their children and teachers ushered students towards the doors. A multitude of knapsacks, bearing the names and the emblems of all the latest fads and interests, swelled together in a rainbow of colours. Those same knapsacks that, over the school year, would become abandoned and lost, tarnished over time, drenched in rainstorms, hurled at enemies, distorted with the weight of books, made smelly with forgotten lunches, or just plain chucked forlornly into the Lost and Found.

Mr. Donlevy held one of the doors open for them to enter. In no way a tall man, Mr. Donlevy could hold himself straight and look like the tallest man in the universe. He had this peculiar way of walking, his shoulders back, but it never seemed fake or overly dramatic.

In some ways, he could be overly dramatic. For as long as Paul could remember, Mr. Donlevy had been the organizer of the Drama Club. Apparently, he was a hit with the kids. Paul had never been interested in drama and had never participated in the club.

Mr. Donlevy had never been Paul or Chad's teacher but he pretty much knew every student in the school. They'd heard exciting things about him: his sense of humour, his energy, his focus on teaching about multiculturalism.

He was also known for wearing a broad-brimmed hat as if he'd just emerged from the Ecuadorian rainforest. He wore the hat, he said, because he had thinning hair on the top of his head and he burned easily.

"Hey, I'm in your class this year," Paul told him as he passed.

He could've said *Cool* but he seemed to be one of the few adults who knew it was *uncool* to say *Cool* in the presence of children and teenagers. "I'm glad, Paul," he said. "We'll have a good year."

Chad said something to him, too, as he went by, and then joined up with Paul. They walked up to their room on the second floor and stood around with mostly familiar students.

There were three grade seven classes in all, one being French Immersion. As things went, Liz happened to be in Mr. Donlevy's class also. She stood talking to Elizabeth Bronson, her best friend. In fact, having been classmates with Elizabeth many times over the years was the reason that Elizabeth Parkinson had shortened her name to Liz. Either one of them could have made the change for neither seemed to mind.

Amid the confusion and noise in the halls, the rising voices of teachers, not yet edgy and still holding some degree of good cheer from the summer, could be heard. Mr. Donlevy appeared and showed them into the room.

They hung up their knapsacks and stood, watching Mr. Donlevy. He said there was no seating plan and allowed them to take any seat they wanted. This led to some excitement as, naturally, they placed themselves next to those they liked the most.

After some fumbling and tumbling over desks, Mr. Donlevy looking on in amusement, they looked around to check out the posters and decorations that Mr. Donlevy had put up. He hadn't resorted to the usual practice of placing grammar rules and number columns in obvious places – at eye level and not to be missed by even the most bored of pupils. Instead, he had strung up posters that advertised well-known books or movies based on books. Some they knew and some they would come to know. There were also posters with interesting proverbs. Mr. Donlevy would discuss them with the students over the course of the year.

He watched them quietly for some time as they fidgeted around in their new seats, trying to find some mode of comfort. When their excitable voices had quietened, he said, "Don't get too delirious about the seating arrangement." That was Mr. Donlevy, Paul would soon learn. Like his dad, he was always pulling out these enormous words to trap them into asking what they meant. "It will change. I like to start the year with the students seated in rows. Then when I have an idea as to who can sit beside who, I can make other arrangements."

"But Mr. Donlevy," said Arif in a falsely innocent tone, "we're already sitting where we want to sit. We swear, we'll never ever give you any trouble this way."

Some students laughed.

"Oh, we'll see about that, Arif. I'll keep you to your word."

Arif looked surprised. "You know my name?"

"There's a lot I know."

"This place is getting spookier by the second," Arif whispered to the boy seated next to him.

"First off, I'd like to welcome everyone back. I hope you had a great summer. Also, I'm glad to be here and I'm glad to have you in my class. We're going to have a good year."

He wrote his name on the board. Then, he grabbed the attendance folder off his desk. "I guess we have to start with introductions. I know this is boring but it's necessary."

Then ensued that hilarious routine in which the teacher manages to mangle and mispronounce half the names on the attendance record. Misinterpreting the silent *g* in Vietnamese names or not knowing that the Chinese *q* sounds like the English *ch*. He did seem to understand the double *l* in Spanish pronunciations.

He also understood the origin of Paul's name. "Brager." He looked at Paul. "Scandinavian, right?"

Paul nodded.

"Norwegian, to be exact."

Paul nodded again.

"Have you a younger brother in the school?"

Paul felt slightly embarrassed. He didn't want anyone to associate him with Adrian. "I...uh...I'm not sure."

Even Mr. Donlevy laughed at this. "Ah yes, the joys of familial relationships."

When he got to Chad's name, he said, "Parlez-vous francais?"

Chad shook his head.

"Isn't *Tremblay* French?"

"Yeah."

"Do you have French background?"

"Well I suppose..." Some laughter. "I mean, it goes back in..."

"Generations," Liz prompted him.

"Yeah...No one in my family speaks French. But my grandparents have a French coat of arms hanging in their living-room."

"Oh, how interesting...What does it show?"

Mr. Donlevy seemed to be genuinely interested. They knew he loved to travel. He was always bringing back fascinating artifacts from his journeys and then using them to connect with a cultural celebration in the school. He always wore a dark red, silk robe during the Chinese New Year. Whenever someone asked him where he bought something, his answer was never *Sears* or *Chinatown* or even *This Egyptian shop on Yonge Street*. It was always *China!* Or *Egypt*. *In this tiny place just off of the Nile!*

They knew he especially loved Mexico.

"Uh," said Chad, "I'm not really sure." More laughter. "I mean, I think it's a French coat of arms."

"Well your job is to ask about it the next time you visit your grandparents. It's important to know about people's histories. As they say, knowing the past aids in helping us avoid problems in the present."

When he asked who wanted to take the attendance down to the office, every single hand went up. The students read the thoughts in the faces of their neighbours: everyone was curious to investigate Theisen and how exactly he would be running things.

"Oh, how curious you are." He chose Sylvia Erskine and Paul.

Sylvia never did say much but Paul guessed that her interest in the new principal got her going because, in the hallway, she couldn't shut up. She asked Paul if he had met him yet.

Paul told her about his and Chad's brief meeting with Theisen earlier.

"He introduced himself to me and my mom this morning."

"What did you think of him?"

"Well, his handshake could kill. He's pretty strong."

"Everyone seems to want to make him into this monster. They think he stole Mr. Myers's job but...he's probably the nicest guy in the world." Paul's strained voice could not conceal the falseness of his words.

They walked into the office. The rooms belonging to the principal and vice-principal were just off to the left. Mrs. Tarnapulsky's was the first one. They could get a pretty good view of her room, the door being open. Mrs. T., as they called her, was perched over her computer, lost in thought.

The principal's room was farther. Although they could see that the door was open, they could see nothing inside the room from their angle. The name plate on the door, the place where Mr. Myers used to display his name, now read *Mr. Theisen*.

Mrs. Franklin, Dorian Heights's long-standing administrative assistant, said, "The routine hasn't changed, folks. The folder goes right there on the counter." By now, she had gotten used to the glances cast down towards that last room. "You're a little early though. You're supposed to bring it after the announcements. Remind...uh...who is your teacher?"

Sylvia walked forward. "It's Mr. Donlevy." When she said the name, they heard the squeaking of Mr. Theisen's chair, almost as if in response to Sylvia's answer. It had been the first sound they'd heard from the silent room.

Sylvia placed the folder next to a couple of others. Apparently, they hadn't been the only early arrivals.

Mrs. T. got up from her desk. "Hi guys," she said. Usually full of energy, spewing electricity into even the shortest of greetings and phrases, she seemed tired today. Her greeting lacked its usual intensity. The two words fell from her lips and crashed to the floor. Back in June, they would have stayed on the air like cartoon bubbles. As she went over to talk to Mrs. Franklin, Sylvia and Paul looked at each other. Paul suspected that Mrs. T. was upset that Mr. Myers was not back, seeing that the two of them had had a good rapport.

They were just about to leave when Theisen came from his office. "Well, well," he said, observing them. He showed them a smile along the thin line of his lips and moved towards them.

Paul felt a sort of panic, as if he had, in some way, invaded Theisen's space. Sylvia felt it, too, although she didn't have to say it. Paul felt it radiating from her there beside him. They went back a step in an oddly choreographed dance.

"Hello."

"You've actually met me," Sylvia said, unable to conceal the nervousness in her voice.

Mr. Theisen was staring at Paul. "Yes, I know. I don't forget easily. I've met you both. It's a principal's duty to know all of his students."

Paul experienced some anger, as if Theisen's sudden ownership of Dorian Heights was a violation of all of them and, in particular, Mr. Myers.

Mrs. T. and Mrs. Franklin had stopped talking and were clearly intrigued by Mr. Theisen and the two students.

"And do you know *all* of the students here?" Paul challenged, a little too boldly.

Sylvia shuddered beside him. He could actually feel her shuddering.

Theisen narrowed his eyes at Paul. "Getting to know them. Before you know it, I will know them. Come boy, this is only the first day. Did you know all the teachers after *your* first day?"

Now it was Paul's turn to narrow his eyes. "It wasn't *my* job to know them."

There was a long silence before Theisen gave a deep, guttural laugh. "You are a clever boy, Paul Brager. Very clever. I like you."

Paul wanted to strike out with his hand and obliterate the stupid, smug grin that wouldn't dissolve. When Paul looked at him, Theisen's eyes pierced him. Paul knew in an instant that Theisen knew his thoughts: that, in a matter of seconds, Paul hated his guts. But also that Paul and he both knew Paul could never defy or outsmart him without being humiliated or hurt in some way.

And no one in that room, it seemed, could say anything at that point. No one was willing to venture a single word. Not a single explanation.

"I think," Mr. Theisen said, "you need to go back to your room now."

Before Paul turned to leave, his eyes caught the big, bloodstone ring on Theisen's finger. It was closer to him than it had been on his first two meetings with the man and as Theisen reached up to scratch his chin, Paul studied the ring. Theisen noticed Paul's curiosity and held his hand steady for awhile so that Paul could take in the engraving. Though set in black, the engraving could still be seen by Paul.

Sylvia and everyone else in the room saw this strange, almost sinister, exchange of wordless information between Mr. Theisen and Paul. Then Paul and Sylvia were in the hall and walking back to their classroom.

"What did you *do* to him?" asked Sylvia.

"What d'ya mean?"

"Well...he seems to have something in for you. And you weren't exactly friendly to him either."

"I don't know. I can't explain. I...uh...I just don't know...You remember Jed Herzog?"

Jed had been in grade eight the year before. He had been well-known as a bully and a constant pain to all the teachers.

"How could I forget him?"

"Well...Remember how he could irritate you...just by giving you that annoying look? Didn't have to touch you or even say anything to you. He just looked at you, tryin' to get you to react. So that when you did react, it would give him an excuse to lace you one."

Sylvia nodded.

"Well that's the way it was just now. It was Jed all over again."

"Jed reincarnated," giggled Sylvia. "And what's with the ring? That black, ugly thing?"

They were now outside their classroom door and they paused.

"I just had to see what was on it."

"Okay. So what was on it?"

"An eagle with its wings outstretched."

Sylvia shrugged. "That doesn't mean anything."

But it would.

* * *

At supper that day, Mr. Brager had to call Paul away from the computer. When Paul arrived in the kitchen, everything was true to the routine. Adrian was very neatly pushed up to the table, studying the fork in his right hand as if it were a million bucks. Brager had on those oversized oven mitts and was taking something steaming and delicious-smelling from the oven.

Paul's mom had always done the cooking and after she died, Brager took over. In the beginning, the meals were simple and bland and sometimes they had to order in. But after five years of practice, he had perfected a lot of the art of cooking, even gauging preparation times to coincide with the boys' homework and free time schedules. His wife would've been proud.

Brager put some garlic bread on the table, warning his sons it was hot but this did not dissuade Adrian who managed to burn his fingers.

Paul chuckled.

"It hurt!" Adrian flung at his brother.

"Don't be so stupid. He told you it was hot."

Adrian put his one finger in his mouth and sucked on it.

Brager put a salad bowl on the table and looked at Paul. "Nothing more. It's over."

"Sure. Right."

Brager put a pan of lasagna on a wooden stand in the middle of the table. He pointed at it. "What's this, Adrian?"

Adrian removed his finger from his mouth. "It's hot," he said sulkily.

Paul helped himself to the salad. "I got to say this, Dad. You're a good cook."

"Is that all you got to say?" Brager grinned.

"Well...uh...what do you want me to say?"

"Nothing. Eat, my son. Then go forth and prosper."

Adrian snickered.

Paul rolled his eyes. He did like his dad, he supposed, and he certainly wouldn't have traded him for Mr. Tremblay. Tremblay might have been crude with his words sometimes but he never said anything corny.

They munched away for awhile before Adrian perked up. "Hey Dad, we gotta new principal. It's on a newsletter but I forgot to bring it home."

"No kidding?" Brager looked at Paul.

"He's kinda weird," Paul said.

"What makes him weird?"

"Well he wears a suit and tie, for one thing."

"Oh yeah, that's weird."

"Well, you know, in this weather..."

"You've got a point."

"Salad, please!"

"...but he's just...It's the way he looks at you." And, by saying that, Paul meant himself, personally. He had never told his father about that day on Centre Island.

"What happened to Mr. Myers? He was such a good principal."

"The kids in my room said he died," blurted Adrian.

"He didn't die, Adrian. Jeez. I don't know, Dad. No one seems to know. The teachers are carrying on like nothing is different."

"So, in fact," Brager said, "being dead is not an impossibility..."

"Well, I guess."

"See!" Adrian said to his brother.

Paul ignored him. "He might've just got transferred."

"True. Let's hope for the best. What's the new principal's name?"

Adrian screwed up his face. "Tree-sun. Somethin' like that."

"No." Paul scowled. "More like...tie-sun."

"Really?" Brager looked genuinely interested and pulled his chair closer to the table. "How do you spell it?"

"You got me," said Adrian, his mouth full.

"I don't know."

Brager pursed his lips. "I suppose it's written on that newsletter Adrian forgot to bring home."

Paul shrugged, his mouth twisting as it fought off the heat from the lasagna.

"I guess you don't have one."

Paul shook his head. "They give one per family. That way, they save paper."

"Makes sense." He touched Adrian's arm. "Try to bring it tomorrow, hmm?"

"Yes sir!" Adrian saluted.

Paul looked at his dad. "What does it matter how he spells his name?"

"Well because if it's T-H-E-I-S-E-N, then it's a Norwegian name. Like ours."

Adrian stopped eating, concentrating on what his father had just spelled.

Mr. Brager was suddenly looking away from the table, his face shadowing with a nervous expression.

Paul thought about the letters that were there on Theisen's door and thought maybe the spelling his father had just done was the correct spelling. Perhaps, Paul wondered, all of this explained why Theisen was so interested in him and that they shared the same ethnicity. This made him feel nauseous. Frankly, he didn't want to share any commonalities with that man. "There's another thing, Dad."

Mr. Brager had difficulty looking at him. "What?"

"I think I've seen him somewhere." *Even before I saw him at Centre Island*, Paul thought.

"Oh? Do you remember where?"

"No but...I have...seen him before. I know I have!"

Mr. Brager suddenly looked worse.

Chapter 4: Mr. Theisen
Plays With Riddles

"If you only had a day left to live, what would you do?" The students were quiet. Mr. Donlevy's question took them by surprise. Usually, they were eager at volunteering answers in Mr. Donlevy's room because he seemed so interested in them; however, since they had all met Mr. Theisen by now, all words, even those uttered by confidants, appeared suspect, out-of-the-ordinary, dangerous. Mr. Donlevy's question could have been a trap, for all they knew.

Mr. Donlevy gave a little laugh. "I'm not trying to get into your personal lives. I'm just following up on yesterday's discussion about sacrifice."

They were reading *The Lion, the Witch, and the Wardrobe* and had gotten to the part where Aslan had sacrificed his life for Edmund in order to appease the White Witch and the laws of Narnia.

Mr. Donlevy had started a discussion about sacrifice and what people were willing to sacrifice or who they were willing to sacrifice it for.

"Perhaps I should ask this differently. If you only had one day to live, what kinds of things would you do? What would you say to friends and family? Or would you? What would you eat as your last meal?"

There was some silence before Arif spoke up. "Does this have anything to do with sacrifice?"

"Not necessarily. Say, perhaps, you had an illness and were told that you only had a day left to live."

"Well I wouldn't come to school, that's for sure." Arif got a few laughs and a few strong agreements.

"Neither would I," said Mr. Donlevy.

"I'd go to Canada's Wonderland," someone said.

"I'd go to Las Vegas," said Michael.

"You'd be dead by the time you got your ticket and travelled there," said Liz. "You're too young to gamble anyway."

Michael blushed. It didn't take much to make him blush.

"I'd steal all the Mars Bars I could and just pig out," said Tony Rappello, a small kid who sat at the back.

"You might get a stomachache," joked Chad, looking back.

"You think I'd care?"

"I suppose I'd tell my family I loved them," said Sylvia, half-serious. She had a younger sister in Adrian's class but, unlike Paul, she did a lot of activities with her sibling. People could see them at the end of the school day, hand-in-hand, walking home. Girls, Paul thought, that's what they do.

"Awwww!" went the class and Sylvia giggled into her hand.

"What about you?" Arif addressed Mr. Donlevy. "What would you do?"

They all became silent again, training their eyes on him. The skin around his eyes crinkled as he thought a bit, then he said, "Well first I would find someone to look after my dog."

"You have a dog?"

"What kind is it?"

"Cocker Spaniel. Mostly white with a few light brown patches."

"Like me," said Arif and everyone laughed.

They knew that Mr. Donlevy was not married, nor ever had been. This conversation had come up about the second week of school when the students were really starting to get curious about him. He only gave so much information, stressing that he was there to teach them, not to be their friend. Not like Miss Nichols, the grade two teacher, who danced with her students in between lessons.

They also knew he had no children. He said something about being "married to travel" and that he travelled whenever he could. Having a wife or kids would have been unfair to them and also to his own interests, he said, because not everyone wanted to travel as much as he did. And if they did, they might prefer destinations different from the ones he preferred. He said he couldn't force a family to go with him only to satisfy his own cravings. Familial harmony took a great deal of work and could not be supported on one person's needs.

Chad said that if his parents had taken him on trips the moment he was born, it would've been cool.

Everyone in the room except for Mr. Donlevy had looked at him strangely. That was Mr. Donlevy: he never treated any of them as stupid or insignificant.

Lots of young people love to travel, too, Mr. Donlevy once said, but they needed to be stable first, to get to know the environment they were born into and establish relationships with their parents. They should not be whisked away without first experiencing their surroundings, he explained.

"What's your dog's name?" asked Tony.

"Beso."

"What?"

"It's Spanish for *kiss*," said Rodrigo who had moved to Canada from Nicaragua two years before.

"Oooohhh," somebody said but was cut short when Liz said, "I like it. I think it's a great name."

Paul was too embarrassed to look back at her. This would have sent a message to everyone in the room. In particular, to Liz who might have been staring at him right now for all he knew.

"Anyway," Arif said, evidently put off by the change in subject, "after you found someone to take care of Beso, what would you do next?"

"I would take a book of poetry by Edgar Allan Poe – he's my favourite writer – to my favourite restaurant and I'd read his poems and eat all day. I'd sit out on the patio if it were a warm day."

Paul could tell by the deflated air in the room that the students were a little disappointed with the response. But, after all, Mr. Donlevy couldn't go to China or Russia or Egypt with one day to spare.

"Would you tell your family?" someone asked.

"He doesn't have a family."

"I mean his mom and dad...Brothers and sisters, you know."

"No...I wouldn't."

"Why not?"

"Hey, that's getting personal."

Mr. Donlevy took a breath. "It just takes up too much time...Explanations often get dragged out...And then there are the reactions from people that come with the explanations...And if I only have one day, I'd rather spend it doing things other than talking..." He looked away from them, flustered, as if he thought he had said too much. "So how does all of this tie in with sacrifice? What would we be willing to sacrifice? Aslan was willing to give up his life just to save a child he hardly knew."

"Well there are small sacrifices and big ones," said Vafa, a Muslim girl who wore a hijab. "Aslan made a big sacrifice."

"Yeah, what could be bigger than dying for somebody?" said Arif but he didn't get the laughs he expected this time.

"Give an example of a small sacrifice," Mr. Donlevy said to Vafa.

Vafa was usually very confident in her opinions and often spoke unreservedly. "Well in my religion, during Ramadan, we make a small sacrifice by giving up food at certain times..."

"Fasting," said Arif, not to be outdone.

Vafa nodded. "We make a promise to not eat certain foods."

"Does everyone know why Vafa does this? Why certain Muslim people do this?" Mr. Donlevy asked the class.

"So they can understand how poor people feel," said Sylvia. "You know, people who don't have a lot of food."

Mr. Donlevy beamed. "Such a smart class."

They laughed.

Vafa's grandparents and father had immigrated to Toronto from Afghanistan over thirty years ago when the then-Soviet Union had invaded her country. Her father had eventually grown up and married a Canadian woman, also of Afghani heritage. Vafa was born in Canada. She was extremely proud of her family's history and was always ready to spar with the ignorant who discriminated against her country and its people. They all admired her not only for her spunk but also because her arguments were reasonable.

"We also celebrate Eid which is a festival of sacrifice," Vafa went on. "It honours Abraham's love of...God...Well, Allah."

"Who?"

"It's in the Bible," one of the girls said a little hesitantly. "I think."

Mr. Donlevy wrote the names *Abraham* and *Isaac* on the board. "These are how the names are spelled in the Christian religion. I am not an expert on religions but I believe they have different spellings according to what religion you are talking about."

Vafa nodded vigorously.

"Oh yeah, I recognize those dudes," Tony said.

"Didn't one of them sacrifice the other?" asked Elizabeth Bronson who had chosen a seat right next to Liz, of course.

Vafa turned around in her seat and they could see that she was anxious to talk. "Actually, God...wanted to see how much Abraham loved him. So He told Abraham to... well, kill his son..."

Paul sat up in his chair, intrigued.

"Isaac was the son..."

"Oh man, could I do that to my brother?"

The comment went ignored.

"So did he?" Liz asked.

"He almost did. But when...God...saw Abraham's..."

"Devotion," offered Mr. Donlevy.

"Yeah...God stopped the sacrifice and let Isaac live."

There was a long silence before Michael said, "So that's what Eid is about?"

"Partly." Vafa saw that she had everyone's attention so she decided to appeal to them on another level. "Some families actually sacrifice a goat or a sheep during Eid."

"You mean...?"

"Yeah, they kill it."

"Ewww..."

"Well, my family doesn't go that far. I know some families do, though. Maybe not so much here in Canada."

"And then...what?"

"They eat it, stupid! What do you think?" said Arif.

"No putdowns," Mr. Donlevy said sternly. These always made him upset. He let conversations go on for long periods of time, unrestricted, but he'd soon intervene if anyone got insulted.

"Ewww..."

"Yeah, like you don't eat hamburgers."

"Actually, I don't."

"You don't eat hamburgers?"

"Okay, we're getting a little off topic here," Mr. Donlevy reminded everyone.

There was another long silence before Michael said, "So, Mr. Donlevy, could you maybe bring in a picture of Beso for us to see?"

But Mr. Donlevy didn't have time to answer because, at that moment, the in-class phone rang. After Mr. Donlevy answered it, he looked over at Paul. "Paul, Mr. Theisen would like to see you in his office. Nothing serious."

It was the first time Paul had ever been in Theisen's office. The first thing he noticed when he came in the room was the big bowl of apples on the desk in front of him. It was so big, in fact, that it seemed to dwarf Paul. Paul thought back to the first time the two of them met and Theisen was chewing away on that apple. He obviously liked them.

Other than the bowl, not much else took up residence on Theisen's desk, not even the ubiquitous family photos. For that matter, Paul didn't know if Theisen had a family. Who would want him, anyway? Paul thought but then reconsidered this as probably just a little too cruel. There was a container full of pens, an open daybook, those kinds of teacherish things.

Theisen greeted him and moved the apples aside so that they could both get a clear view of each other.

"Now, as you know, Paul, I want to get to know all the students under my care. I think that's important. That's what this is all about."

"You have a big job if you're doing this with every single student in Dorian Heights." But as far as Paul was aware, no one else in his room had had this privilege ... yet.

Theisen chuckled. "I can handle it...Anyway, it won't take up too much of your time." Very officially, he took out a file folder and put it on the desk in front of him. "I've been looking through your OSR." When he saw Paul's confused look, he added, "Ontario Student Record. It goes with you wherever you go. If you change schools, for instance..."

"Oh yeah. Is that the thing with all my report cards and all the bad things I've done in school?"

Theisen grinned. "Come, Paul. We both know how well you've done in school. Nothing to be ashamed of in your case."

In *his* case. Not like in *Tony's* case where, last year, he had got into that fight with a kid from another school and was suspended for three days.

Paul suddenly felt violated, as if Theisen was sneaking into their houses and going through their personal items. Was he going to comment on the fight when he had Tony there in his office? How far would he go? How much would he say? Mr. Myers would never have set up these conferences.

"So your brother, Adrian, is in Mrs. Wanamaker's room..."

Paul nodded.

Theisen looked down at the folder. "Your dad is... Fredrik Brager..."

Here, Paul shifted, noticeably uncomfortable. *Don't say a thing about my mom*, he thought, *don't say a thing*. His jaw hurt and he finally understood that this was because he was clenching his teeth.

Theisen seemed to read his mind and closed up the folder.

The thing about Paul's memory of his mother was this: he had never let go but he could never really talk about it either. His anger wasn't only directed at Theisen. It was directed at anyone who cared to mention his mother, even the people who were trying to help him. One day, he'd get over it, he knew, but when would that be?

Theisen crossed his arms. "How is school going for you this year so far, Paul?"

"It's okay. I mean, it just started." Paul looked around behind him. Theisen had left the office door open. Teachers needed to do these things these days as much to protect themselves as to protect the kids. So neither could be accused of anything. Paul was kind of glad the door was open.

"You like it here at Dorian Heights?"

"Sure. I've been here a long time." Paul didn't want to volunteer too much information.

Theisen squirmed a bit. His expression was hard to read, as if he had something very important to say. "Uh, Paul..."

"Yes?"

"I have something to discuss with you but...I don't know if...Well, it concerns your father."

Paul took on a defensive look before he even realized it was there.

Mr. Theisen put his hands up as if he wanted Paul to relax. "You see, Paul, I think I know your father."

Paul sat up. "Oh?"

"Your father is the real reason I've called you here."

"How do you know him?"

Theisen said nothing but he looked as if he were wondering how he should formulate his words. "You might say we met in the past."

Paul wondered if this is how he recognized Mr. Theisen from somewhere: perhaps seeing him meeting with Paul's dad. Yet Paul's dad had not said anything about knowing Mr. Theisen when Adrian mentioned their new principal.

"Your father and I used to...well, I guess....You see, we used to play games together when we were young...When we were children."

Paul was doubtful. "Did you go to the same school?"

Theisen shook his head.

"Were you neighbours?"

Theisen grinned but Paul didn't like the grin: it appeared to be slightly malicious. "I guess you could call us that. Your father would agree we were neighbours."

Paul thought that Theisen was deliberately trying to be mysterious.

"We played this one game, you see. It was like a treasure hunt. Each of us had to hide an object and the other had to find it. Whoever found it first was the winner."

Paul wanted to scream out, *Why are you telling me this? What does this have to do with school?* But he couldn't. He was strangely fascinated with Theisen's words, almost hypnotized.

"Only guess what, Paul? The hidden objects were apples."

"Apples?"

"Only apples."

Iduna's apples, Iduna's apples automatically ran through Paul's head. He looked up and saw Theisen smiling. "Why apples?"

"Well, your father and I saw them as...more precious than rubies...I bet you see the significance in that, hmm? Children like to use one thing to represent another... Especially when you can't afford the other."

Paul was thinking hard about what to say, not wanting to get too chummy with this man. "Did you...uh...like the game?"

"Ask your father that, Paul. Ask him if he liked the game."

Paul stood up.

"Oh Paul, there's another thing."

Paul thought, *Is he going to reveal some secret about my dad? Is that what this is all about?*

"Your father and I pretended the apples gave us tremendous strength...You know, muscles, for example."

Paul eyed the bowl of apples on the desk. "Is that why you eat those?"

Theisen put his head back and laughed. "You could say that. Apples benefit us in many ways."

Paul shuffled his feet. "Uh..."

"I've kept you here far too long, Paul. It was good to talk to you. You can return to your class."

Paul stood up and was about to leave but then turned. "Mr. Theisen."

"Hmmm?"

"Do you think he'll remember you?"

Theisen smiled. "Oh I think he'll remember me quite well."

Out in the hall, Paul thought about the odd exchange he had just had with Theisen.

It started to make him feel uncomfortable.

Why would Theisen still be interested in a foolish game played years ago? In a sense, Paul believed, Theisen was playing some kind of game with him, too.

Paul also felt wary for his father. He did believe there was some connection between him and Theisen but what it was, he could not comprehend. Was his dad in some kind of trouble? Was Theisen using riddles to torment him in some way?

Paul's discomfort turned into anger and he almost charged back into the office and confronted Theisen, demanding the truth. But he got hold of himself. He needed to think this through.

One thing he was sure of: he wasn't ready to disclose any of this to anyone. He'd wait that out a little.

Theisen had rattled him but Paul would get over it.

Chapter 5: Inside Mr. Donlevy's Condo

The small, framed picture of Beso sat up on Mr. Donlevy's desk the way that other teachers had pictures of their spouses or children, decked out in ski gear on a mountain or clad in beachwear somewhere in the Caribbean. Reminders, Paul supposed, that there were other places more important than their jobs.

Mr. Donlevy was also in the picture. He and Beso sat on a wooden bench outside, greenery all around them, as they stared in a relaxed manner at the camera. Mr. Donlevy had his arms folded, looking cool in a T-shirt and shorts while Beso, beside him, seemed a little more wary of this strange thing taking his picture. His ears looked cocked in that comical way dogs have of showing confusion or curiosity.

The first day the picture came out, they all gathered around and took turns looking at it, telling Mr. Donlevy how cute his little, fuzzy dog was. They were also anxious for any clues in the photo that would tell them more about Mr. Donlevy but they didn't have a lot to go on. The picture had obviously been taken in late spring or summer. Mr. Donlevy looked a little younger, his hair not as short as it was now. The bench on which the two were sitting, Beso's paws curled just over the edge of it, was in the garden that Mr. Donlevy used to own. He had sold his house two years ago and he and Beso now lived in a condo on the harbourfront.

Always intent on being a detective, Arif asked who had taken the picture.

"My mother."

"You have a mother?" asked Michael and they all rolled their eyes.

The longer the photo sat on the desk, the less they became interested in it, giving it a passing glance now and then when they walked by.

One day, early in October, when Paul and Chad were in no hurry to get home after school and they had no club commitments, Mr. Donlevy asked them to stay. He had something important to ask them.

"I'll get right to the point. I'm going away over Thanksgiving. I leave directly from here on Friday to catch my flight."

"Where ya going?" Chad asked.

"Always curious," snickered Mr. Donlevy. "New York City."

"Wow. I always wanted to go there."

Paul gave Chad a puzzled look. Chad had never ever told him he wanted to go there. "Since when?"

Chad couldn't mask his embarrassment. "I don't know...Since I started liking the Rangers, I guess." Chad sent back a *Don't push it!* look. After all, Paul hadn't been exactly forthright with him either. That day after seeing Theisen in the office, Paul had been very limited in telling Chad what Theisen had said to him. And Paul knew Chad was cheesed off about it. The fact is, he wasn't sure how to broach the subject to Chad.

Interestingly, when Paul had asked his classmates if Theisen had sat down with them yet, no one said he had.

Mr. Donlevy seemed amused by the exchange between the two boys. "Anyway, this brings me to the situation of Beso."

Both Paul and Chad sat up. "You want us to take care of him?" Paul asked, an edge of excitement in his voice. Now it was his turn to be embarrassed.

"Hold on, hold on. Don't get too excited. I usually ask my mother to look after him when I go away."

Paul was sure Chad was thinking the same thing as he right then: why didn't he ever mention a father?

"She can on Saturday, Sunday, and Monday. Trouble is she has another commitment on Friday evening and wouldn't be able to take him then. You see, she usually keeps him at her place. She can come and get him Saturday morning, no problem...I basically need someone to come and feed him around five or six and take him for a walk...Then another walk around ten o'clock. That should make him okay until my mother comes early to get him on Saturday."

Paul and Chad looked at each other, then Paul said, "So you actually want us to come into your...condo?"

"Well unless Beso develops some kind of magic in which he can jump out the keyhole."

They laughed.

"No, I mean..."

"You'd have to speak to your parents, of course. In fact, I wouldn't want you coming alone...Especially at ten in the evening...I know you're in grade seven...I know you're both responsible..."

"Yeah, we get it," Chad said. "I think...my parents... would say it's okay."

"You don't seem so sure about that."

Chad swallowed. "Well, I'll just ask."

"Neither of you is going anywhere Friday? Going away for Thanksgiving?"

They shook their heads.

"If your parents say it's okay, I'll have you over some time before Friday so you can get to meet Beso...And get to know the building. I'll introduce you to the concierge."

"The what?"

"The guy who does security," Paul told Chad.

"Can you let me know tomorrow?"

They nodded and got up.

"One more thing, guys."

They waited.

"I don't want this thing to turn into a 'teacher's pet' situation...I'm sure you wouldn't want that either...The fact is, I need someone I can trust to take care of Beso on Friday. I could have chosen plenty of students from this classroom...So why you two? Because I needed a team...It's better safety-wise when there are two of you together...And you two are about the strongest examples of friendship in this classroom. You two seem to rely on each other."

Paul and Chad exchanged silly grins before Chad said, "Elizabeth and Liz are a pretty good team."

Mr. Donlevy nodded. "Absolutely, but..." He mulled over his choice of words. "It just wouldn't be right. A male teacher asking two female students to come into his condo. It's just the times we live in, guys."

"We get it," Paul said. "You have to be careful."

"I try to treat all of you equally," Mr. Donlevy went on. "So don't see this as favouritism...You just, as I said, make a good team...Also, most of the time, I do things alone...I like being alone...Outside of the class, I mean. I don't invite a lot of people to come into my living space. It's where I go to get away from everything. But I also can't be ridiculous about this. Obviously, if I choose to go on trips, I'm going to need to rely on people to take care of Beso."

Paul thought he saw where this conversation was going but wasn't really sure. "Is there something in your condo you want us to stay away from, Mr. Donlevy?"

Chad cast him a strange look. "Don't sound so spooky, man."

"Of course not," Mr. Donlevy laughed. "I just want to ask you to respect my personal space. You can look around and ask questions while you're there. Just don't talk about things to anyone else. Keep it private."

Chad nodded slowly but Paul sensed his body going rigid with tension beside him.

"Don't worry. I don't have a torture chamber..."

"I think I understand," Paul said. "Just like if we asked you to keep something private. You'd respect that too, wouldn't you, Mr. Donlevy?"

"Of course."

Chad looked over at Paul. "You got something to share with us, Brager?"

They all laughed.

No, thought Paul, now wasn't the time, not for both of them to hear at once. There'd be too many questions, too many suggestions.

Paul and Chad had already imagined that Mr. Donlevy's condo was full of antiques, paintings, and possessions from the many places he had travelled. He simply didn't want the two of them taking back information to the others. It would be an invasion of privacy. People like Arif would get way out of hand.

"To tell you the truth," Paul said, wanting to sound responsible, "I wouldn't even tell the others we took care of Beso...Like you said, they would all start seeing us as teacher's pets."

"Yeah," Chad agreed.

"I think that's wise," Mr. Donlevy said. "Okay, let me know tomorrow. And...thanks."

"Hey Dad, what's the treasure?"

Mr. Brager, Paul, and Adrian had just sat down for supper, the chili still steaming in the bowl.

Brager pulled himself up in his chair and looked at Adrian who had a silly grin on his face.

"What?"

"What's the treasure?"

"I don't know what you mean." Brager looked at Paul, whose horrified expression resembled his own.

Not long after his interview with Theisen, Paul had been approached twice by the man to see if Paul had mentioned their meeting to Paul's father. The first time Paul answered no, Theisen got paler but shrugged it off. The second time, Theisen showed an angry expression and stomped off.

Paul should have known that the skunk would have gotten impatient and appealed to the next possible resource: Adrian.

His father actually looked shaken. This is what Paul was afraid of.

"You used to go on treasure hunts when you were young, right? When you were my age?"

"Shut up, Adrian," Paul said through clenched teeth but his brother, all innocence, didn't understand what he was putting his father through. Paul looked at his dad. "He's been talking to Mr. Theisen."

"Oh?"

Adrian stared, open-mouthed, at Paul. "How'd you know?"

Paul said nothing, his face red.

Brager looked at Paul. "Theisen? The principal?"

Paul nodded.

"Has Theisen been talking to you as well?"

Paul nodded again.

"Hey! This is my game!"

"Go ahead," Paul said to Adrian, "tell Dad what the treasure is."

Brager looked at Adrian, his face softening. "Go ahead, kid."

"Okay. Here, Dad, I'll give you some clues. Shiny and...uh...red...and...No...Okay, that's it! Shiny and red!"

"Those are all the clues? That's it?"

Adrian shook his head wildly.

"So the treasure is supposed to be shiny...and red?"

More wild nodding.

"And the treasure gives you strength, Dad. It gives you strength," Paul threw in.

After some thought, Brager threw down his hands and began serving the chili. "I give up. What is it?"

Adrian was disappointed. "No, you tell me! You're supposed to know!"

Uhh, thought Paul, that's how Theisen had set this up with Adrian: as if they were playing their own game.

"Son, calm down...Now, listen. *I'm* supposed to know what the treasure is?"

"Yeah...and *where* it is. So where is it?"

Brager looked back at Paul. "And Theisen told you I know about this treasure?" He was looking faint.

"He said..." Paul started, then cleared his throat. "He said that he knew you when you were younger. When you were kids, I guess."

"From where?"

Paul went on with the entire conversation between Theisen and him. By the time he got to the end, Adrian was sufficiently bored and had decided to pick away at his chili.

Brager had gone quite white and was gripping the table to steady himself.

"Dad, was he lying? Did you know each other?"

"Uh...Yes, yes...Of course." But he didn't say this very convincingly.

"Then what is the treasure, Dad? What's he talking about? He said apples but he said they were...well, *precious* to both of you. Does he mean they were more than just apples? Like in the story you told Adrian?"

Adrian perked up again, studying his dad's face. "Ohhh...Apples. I get it." But he made no reference to the story.

Brager said nothing.

"Okay, Dad. It's okay. If it's private, I understand. You don't have to say."

"Oh Paulll..."

Brager managed a smile. "The truth is, son, and I'm going to be frank with you, Mr. Theisen and I did know each other. We did play a kind of game and it did involve apples. And..." His face looked pale. He looked at Paul's face and motioned his head towards Adrian who was looking somewhere else.

Paul nodded in understanding. "Was the game... dangerous?"

Brager put a finger to his lips.

"What?" spluttered Adrian, interested again. "What's dangerous?"

"Eating an apple with a worm in it," said Paul, impressing himself with his quick response.

"Ewww...So what's Mr...Tie...Tie-son talking about, Dad?"

Brager looked exasperated.

"Obviously, he can't talk about it," Paul told Adrian, an edge of irritation in his voice.

"Have you spoken to anyone else about this?"

"No."

Brager sighed. "I am annoyed at Theisen. How dare he use you two to...?" Paul and Adrian looked over at him like hungry dogs watching their master prepare a meal for them. "I will speak to him about this. About his oh-so important little treasure."

Paul could see that Theisen's apparent game was much more serious than imagined.

"Listen, this Theisen doesn't seem trustworthy to me. If he wants you to come into his office again, tell him you won't unless I am there with you...Is that too difficult? I know I'm asking you..."

"I can do it, Dad," Paul said.

"But," said Adrian, "what if he forces us to?"

"He can't do that, Adrian." Brager looked at Paul. "You can trust Mr. Donlevy, right?"

Paul nodded.

"Well if you ever feel threatened, get his help. I'll be seeing him soon, anyway. Interviews are coming up."

Two days before Mr. Donlevy left for his trip, Chad's father chauffeured the boys to Mr. Donlevy's condo. After parking, Mr. Tremblay decided to wait in the lobby while the boys went to the top floor to see Mr. Donlevy.

Mr. Donlevy had forewarned the concierge, Chris, that two students would be coming to see him and to let them into the building.

"He must have a lot of money," Paul whispered to Chad in the elevator, wondering if the cameras could pick up his words. He was thinking, not having had this experience before, that his words were somehow going through a monitor into Mr. Donlevy's own condo.

Chad nodded, amazed by the elevator.

They weren't stupid. They knew what an elevator looked like. They just hadn't had many opportunities to ride in them.

The hallway was carpeted and quiet as they stepped into it. The atmosphere forced them to be silent. They knew they weren't in the middle of a busy intersection of hallways like at Dorian Heights. They tiptoed like Hansel and Gretel to number seven, Mr. Donlevy's door.

Before they could even knock, there was a short, sharp bark on the other side. Then, after their knock, a series of warning but non-threatening yips. They heard Mr. Donlevy scolding Beso in a gentle tone and as he let them in, Beso came bounding forward and jumped up on them playfully. Just like that. No sniffing. Just this immediate greeting, telling them they had passed the test and yes, okay, they had his permission to look after him.

"He has a good sense of smell," Mr. Donlevy said. "Well, he likes you. That's a good thing."

Both Paul and Chad tried not to be girly and make a big deal about Beso's affection. But it was too hard to resist. He kept jumping forward, his stub of a tail wiggling wildly. They ruffled his ears and bent down, almost banging their heads together, letting him lick their faces. His face was furry, his black nose stuck in the middle of all the white, his tiny, brown eyes almost hidden by clumps of hair.

"He needs a haircut. I was waiting to get this weekend out of the way first. He doesn't need extra stress."

"Hi Beso, hi buddy!" Chad said, not too interested in Mr. Donlevy or his words at the moment.

Beso finally stopped jumping but he rubbed his side against their shins and kept looking up and wagging his tail whenever they stopped petting him. Then he would dance around them frantically.

"He's telling you he wants out. To smell the neighbourhood. He thinks you're going to take him out."

Paul gave Mr. Donlevy a questioning look.

"Don't worry, Paul. I've taken him already. He's a real con artist...Nice try, Beso."

Beso responded to his name and walked over to Mr. Donlevy who held out his hand. "Well, welcome boys."

It was then that they looked around. They were in a large living-room. A huge rug, maybe Persian, Paul didn't know, ran the length of the laminate floor. It was wine-coloured with splotches of black, white, and blue, and there were all kinds of designs woven into it. Flowers and interlocked circles. Stuff like that. To their right was a massive chest of drawers, the wood dark, the legs sprouting lions' claws, the top supported by pillars carved like the stems of flowers. To their left was a fireplace, its mantel holding a huge chandelier that had a bronze angel attached to its bottom.

"This place is cool," Chad couldn't help saying. He was looking at an oil painting in an oval frame, just to the side of the chest. There was a man in it, dressed in what looked like the robe of an ancient king, standing proudly for what would become his portrait. "That must be worth a fortune."

"Not really," said Mr. Donlevy.

"How much...?"

"I don't really know, Chad. I never had it evaluated."

"But...you bought it."

"Actually, I inherited it from an uncle. He knew I loved it. I couldn't take my eyes off it whenever I visited him. Just like what you're doing now."

"It must be...jeez, maybe a million."

"I don't really care what it's worth, Chad. In dollar value, I mean." When Chad looked at him, not understanding, he added, "Its real worth is in how much I enjoy looking at it. If you like paintings, you may understand this more as you get older."

"I...I guess so."

Their eyes were all over the place when Mr. Donlevy said, "You two didn't come alone, did you?"

Chad was too enthralled to speak so Paul said, "No. Chad's dad brought us. He's waiting in the lobby." Paul thought Mr. Donlevy might ask Chad to tell his father to come up but he only nodded and remained silent. He guessed that the less people who saw his place, the better. But Paul knew he'd be telling his dad about the place anyway. Chad probably wouldn't peep a word to his dad until his dad started asking questions, those nosy little questions that adults sometimes try to masquerade as sincere interest.

They were offered a drink and a snack but knew they wouldn't be there long and said no.

Just when Beso had stretched out comfortably at Mr. Donlevy's feet, Mr. Donlevy showed them around and this got Beso up again and following them.

It was a big condo, thirteen hundred square feet, they were told, but Mr. Donlevy kept them away from a couple of rooms, one of which must have been his bedroom. He didn't tell them not to enter the rooms. Their shut doors were warning enough.

He spent little time showing them the dining-room, kitchen, and bathroom. They'd already investigated the living-room. He pointed out where Beso's dog food was, where his leash was, and so on. He showed them how to unlock and lock the door and told them to pick up the key from Chris and to leave it again with Chris so that Mr. Donlevy's mother could get it the next day. He also gave them Chris's phone number downstairs in case they had to contact him from within the condo.

"I'll show you where I walk Beso," he said and as he put on his shoes and took up Beso's leash, Beso started twirling in circles, making all of them laugh. Mr. Donlevy had to calm Beso with his words in order that Beso stay still enough to let the leash be attached to his collar. "Other than his excitement about going out, I can't see you having any problems with him. Just in case, I do have the vet's name and office number on the fridge."

As they walked to the elevator, Paul asked how old Beso was.

"Nine."

In the lobby, Chad introduced Mr. Donlevy to his dad. Aside from a couple of phone conversations with Mr. Donlevy, Mr. Tremblay only knew what he was like through Chad's words. And knowing Chad's relationship with his father, that wouldn't have been much.

Paul found the meeting between the two men intriguing. Mr. Donlevy was endeavouring to be amiable and Mr. Tremblay looked very uncomfortable, avoiding the other man's eyes and stumbling over his chipped words and phrases. It was obvious both men had absolutely nothing in common but at least Mr. Donlevy was putting in an effort. When Paul looked at Chad, Chad seemed as edgy as his father.

Mr. Donlevy then had a few words with Chris about the routine on Friday.

Mr. Tremblay decided to remain in the lobby as Mr. Donlevy took the boys outside and across Queens Quay Avenue to get to the park. "I like this park," he told them. "It's one of the more interesting ones. It's well-lit at night and I've never had a problem with strange people. I think you'll be okay walking him here."

They were right next to the harbour. Again, Paul and Chad were captivated. There were a number of boats in various sizes docked nearby.

"Do you have a boat, Mr. Donlevy?"

"No. I like being on them but I don't want to be the captain." His attention went back to Beso. "You'll find that Beso will pee quite soon after you bring him out..."

Paul and Chad had already figured they'd be picking up poop but, having met Beso, there seemed to be nothing that dog could have done to disgust them.

And that was their introduction to Beso and what they'd be doing.

Although his dad agreed to letting Paul look after Beso on the Friday night, he did show some reluctance. Paul knew his dad liked Mr. Donlevy. Paul figured his dad just didn't like seeing the independence his son was gaining. It was a slight change in Paul's life that his dad probably wasn't ready for. Sure, he wanted Paul to make a smooth transition from boyhood to adulthood. It just made aging all the faster for both of them, Paul thought.

His dad said he could drive Chad and him to the condo. Since Mr. Brager could not get out of work until five o'clock, Paul and Chad stuck around at school to shoot some hoops outside while they waited.

When he arrived, he greeted the boys and asked them how their day had been. It was difficult for them to hide their excitement about both the holiday and seeing the condo again.

As he was driving, Paul's dad asked, "So I have to be driving westbound on Queens Quay to get into the entrance?" He had already asked this ten minutes before and probably just wanted to fill the air with conversation.

Paul nodded. He had a good sense he knew where they were going anyway. Every so often his father would look up and out of the windshield and comment how Mr. Donlevy had found himself a real nice area, real nice.

Chad pointed out the Rogers Centre and the CN Tower as they drove by. Both boys had been in them once. Together, of course. The Rogers Centre with Paul's dad to see a Jays game and the CN Tower on a class trip in grade three.

"He's lucky to live so close to them," Chad mentioned to Paul, repeating what he said the other night, the night his father had quipped, "I don't think luck has much to do with it," an edge to his voice.

They turned south on a street that took them to Queens Quay, then turned around and made their way west.

When they got to the building, Paul's dad buzzed in and Paul and Chad recognized Chris's voice on the intercom. Paul's dad looked at him. "You know him. Maybe you should talk."

Feeling important, Paul leaned across his dad and told Chris they had arrived. Chris activated the garage door so they could drive down to the underground parking.

Mr. Brager, as Chad's father had done, chose to wait in the lobby but for a reason distinct from Mr. Tremblay's decision. He knew that the boys were mature enough to go about the duty they had been assigned. His hovering presence would only have irritated them.

Adrian, who was spending the night at the home of his best friend, Stewart, was of a different nature than Paul. He would have insisted that his father accompany him, not so much for safety reasons but simply because, ever since the death of his mother, his father's nearness comforted him. Or maybe because he believed that, if he weren't looking, his dad might disappear, too.

Paul and Chad greeted Chris, picked up the key, and started for the elevator.

"You think that your dad will walk with us in the park at ten?" Chad saw the grin that spread across Paul's face. "I'm not scared. I was just wondering."

In fact, Paul had wondered, too.

Paul still sensed his dad was uncomfortable about his burgeoning independence. Probably because, like most parents, he saw the aging of his child as a reflection of his own aging. And Paul was beginning to understand that getting older was not always a good thing.

Beso gave a bark before they unlocked the door. But this time it sounded fuzzy; as if their approach had roused him from a deep sleep. They opened the door slowly, knowing he was on the mat on the other side of the door. His vantage-point, Mr. Donlevy had told them. No one could enter or leave the place without Beso being aware.

Beso jumped on them. They put their hands down and let him lick them. They looked around quickly at the surroundings, now familiar. Mr. Donlevy had left a note on the chest, welcoming them and inviting them to help themselves to anything in the fridge. There was also a little blurb about leaving a light on for Beso before they left.

"Come on," Chad said as Paul took too much time surveying the note, "he's going to pee himself."

After a quick introduction of Mr. Brager and Beso, the two boys went outside.

Beso didn't wait until the park to pee. A few seconds after they had gone out the front door of the building, he cocked his leg against a cement planter.

Chad laughed and Paul told him he'd do it too if he'd been saving it all day.

Not seeming to mind the huge puddle he'd left on the walkway, Beso pattered ahead happily, leading them to the park.

They probably spent more time in the park than they should have but they were so caught up in seeing people work away on their boats, perhaps getting them ready to sail one more time before the harsh weather, that they had to remind themselves that Paul's dad was waiting for them. They kind of wished he wasn't so that they could spend more time there.

Back in the condo, Paul told Chad to feed Beso as, this time, Paul had to use the washroom. When he came out, Beso was lapping up his food but something was not quite right with the condo. "Chad," Paul said, "what are you doing, man?"

For he had entered one of the rooms they had no business being in.

"Just looking. Not doing anything wrong."

It looked like a study. There was a big, wooden desk in the middle of it, a bookshelf against the wall, a computer in one corner, and an armchair in another. There were more paintings and a photo of Mr. Donlevy on the stern of a boat, his back to the camera, his hair ruffled in the wind, and jagged rocks growing out of the water in front of him.

Chad was poised over the desk. "Where d'ya think that picture was taken?"

"I don't know...and I guess we can't ask him." Paul looked at him like a scolding parent. "Why'd you come in here?"

"I was curious. Like you aren't!"

"Man, be careful what you touch. We have to leave everything exactly the way it was."

"I haven't touched anything...yet." He reached down and tried to open one of the drawers in the desk. It wouldn't budge.

"Chaaaddd..."

"You think he dusts for fingerprints?" he asked mischievously, then tried to open all the other drawers. "This is real mysterious...All of them are locked."

"What's so mysterious about that? You don't lock away things? Like your graphic novels?"

He looked around him. "Where d'ya think he keeps the key? D'ya think he carries it around with him?"

"Let's go. Dad's waiting." Paul figured that if it had been Chad's dad waiting in the lobby, Chad would have insisted they leave long ago.

Chad started picking up things, lamps and such, and then being careful to put them back where he had found them.

"You think he'd be so obvious?"

"Come on, Brager. This is an adventure. Maybe Mr. Donlevy has a secret life."

"Why don't you go and check out the other room?"

"It's only his bedroom. There's nothing very interesting in it."

Paul looked at him in amazement. "You watch too many spy movies, Tremblay."

Now he was down on his hands and knees, looking under the desk and under the computer table, feeling around and along the bottoms.

"Here," Paul said, half-curious and half-angry. He gave him the key to the condo. "When you're ready, you lock up. I'll be waiting with my dad." Then Paul took in the bookshelf and noticed one book in particular.

"Okay, okay, man. Okay." Chad stood up quickly, almost banging his head on the desk. He caught Paul's stare and looked over at the shelf. "What? Do you see it?" He walked over.

"No, no. Let's go." Paul turned.

"What? Come on, Brager. Something spooked you."

But Paul was on his way out the door.

They gave Chris the key and told him they'd be back later.

"Wow," said Mr. Brager. "That took awhile."

"It takes up more time than we thought. By the time we got up to the top floor..."

"Yeah." Chad took over. "There are three elevators but you have to wait forever..."

"Okay, got it," Brager said, grinning. "I'm not angry."

Paul cleared his throat. "I guess we did take up a lot of time in the park. Watching the boats."

"I would have, too," Brager said.

Paul peered at Chad who was in the back seat, looking as guilty as Paul felt, knowing they had somehow violated Mr. Donlevy's life and, in the process, made themselves untrustworthy.

"So what's his place like?"

"Not very interesting," Paul said, trying to hide the falseness in his tone. He was afraid that if his dad kept asking questions, he might lead them into revealing their actions.

In fact, after their episode, the boys were very limited in their descriptions of the place.

"Big screen T.V.?" chuckled Brager.

Paul shared a look of total surprise with Chad. They hadn't even noticed a television in the condo.

"No big-screen T.V.," said Chad when they made their return visit that evening. There was a second chest, more modern-looking and less imposing than the first one, in the living-room. When Chad opened the front doors on it, there was a 20-inch Hitachi staring out at them. "That thing must be ancient."

"Like everything else in here."

They had just walked Beso who had gotten used to following them everywhere and they filled his water bowl. Their walk had still been interesting, even if Paul's dad had walked with them this time. Paul thought it might have had something to do with the darkness settling in although Mr. Brager said he just wanted to stretch his legs and take in the view.

The moon had been out and had shone a path of light across the harbour. Paul's dad remarked again about how lovely this area was.

After the walk, he waited again in the lobby.

In Mr. Donlevy's condo, it was Chad's turn to be startled when, upon coming out of the washroom, he found Paul in the computer room with a book in his hand. "Uh-huh," he said, "I knew it."

Paul grinned. "How many books do you think he has here?"

Chad ignored the question, his eyes on the book that Paul was holding. "Is that what you saw when we were here earlier?"

Paul nodded.

Chad came closer. "*The Illustrated Book of Norse Mythology*," he read, then looked at the bookshelf. "He's got a lotta books on mythology...From all different countries..."

Paul nodded again.

"So why is that one so interesting?"

"Well..." Paul sat in the armchair. "Dad always reads or tells a story to us...to Adrian before he goes to sleep..."

"A bedtime story?"

"Kinda...It's to relax...Adrian. You know? So he won't have any nightmares."

"Isn't he a little old...?" Chad started, then looked embarrassed. "Oh...I get it." Five years ago when they were in grade two, the boys had started their friendship: a simple development that had arisen when Paul had told Chad about the death of his mother. Chad, of course, was still too young to understand completely what empathy was but he knew enough that Paul might feel better if he was invited over to Chad's house for supper. The camaraderie blossomed from there.

Even back in that time, Paul could remember Chad's father as being a grump who tried to cheer everyone with his heavy-handed sarcasm. At least Mrs. Tremblay seemed considerate and well-meaning. She just looked away when her husband tried to be funny.

"So did he read you stories about Norse mythology?"

"Yeah. I think partly because we're Norwegian anyway."

"Oh yeah. That's right."

Paul was fingering through the book. "But I think there's another reason." Paul found a page and started to read to himself.

Chad waited until Paul had been quiet for awhile. "So you wanna tell me?"

"Uh...Just let me read a bit...and then I'll talk about it."

"Yessir!" Chad saluted. "You don't seem so concerned about your dad waiting tonight." When Paul said nothing, Chad resumed his search for the key. He went to the bookshelf, took out the first book on the top shelf, fanned its pages, then shook it until the dust flew. He then held it upside down and shook it again, then held it on its side, the spine at the top, and shook it one more time. He then put it back and repeated his actions with the next book.

Naturally, Paul's attention fell on him. "What on earth are you doing?"

Chad's eyes got wide. "Maybe he has a secret compartment in one of the books and he hides it in there."

"Yeah, okay. And maybe it's buried under the floor."

"Maybe."

Paul rolled his eyes. "Listen, I'm reading a story here and it's very short. I'll give us both five minutes and then we'd better go."

"I can't find it in five minutes."

"Maybe that's best anyway."

Chad scowled, working away at the books. "You probably found it already and won't tell me. You probably found it in..." He squinted. "...in *The Illustrated Book of Norse Mythology.*"

"Shhh..."

"Man, it could be behind one of the books, too." Chad pulled out the books he had just finished inspecting and peered behind them. "Man, I'll never find it. Come and help...Oh, never mind." Exasperated, he straightened the books and planted himself on the carpet. He pulled up an area of carpet that was not held down by something heavy. Of course, Beso had come in and situated himself on a portion of rug that Chad wanted to look under. Chad tried to coax him out of his lying position but Beso, almost mockingly, settled into his spot, put his head on his paws, and watched him contentedly.

"Okay, okay, Beso...You win."

Paul thumped the book down on his lap. To Chad, his face appeared twisted, out of proportion. "Let's go," he said.

"What's wrong?"

"We...Well, we have to go...Dad's waiting." Paul started out the door.

"Yo Brager! The book!"

Paul seemed confused, then realized he was carrying the book. He avoided Chad's stare as he resituated it on the bookshelf.

"You get weird sometimes, Brager. Real weird."

When they were in the elevator, Paul finally found a steady voice. "The story I read in there..." Chad nodded.

"It's...Well, it's one of the stories that Dad...Well, he doesn't read it...He tells it. He doesn't even have a book in front of him when he tells it...He knows it off by heart."

"That's not so strange."

The elevator stopped at the lobby.

"I'll tell you about it on Tuesday," Paul said out of the corner of his mouth as his dad appeared in front of them.

"How was he?"

"Oh...Uh...okay. He started crying a bit when we shut the door. Mr. Donlevy said to expect that, though. That he cries every time Mr. Donlevy leaves for work. We gave him water, we left the light on. Mr. Donlevy's mom comes at six in the morning. He's okay." But somehow Paul felt that he and Chad had neglected Beso when they had found the computer room more interesting.

Chapter 6: Footsteps in the Basement

At school the following Tuesday, Mr. Donlevy gave them each an envelope when no other students were around and told them not to open them until they got home. Beso was fine, he told them, and he had had a wonderful trip.

Paul and Chad couldn't stop laughing about their strange adventure in the condo. Paul kept saying that something horrible could have happened. What if, for example, Beso had taken on the personality of a vicious, snarling killer dog when Chad had tried to get him to shift from the carpet? What if he had leapt on Chad and savaged him to the point where Chad was left mauled and bleeding, the blood spilling out onto the carpet? They pictured themselves phoning 911 or scrubbing the carpet pathetically to get the stains out.

How would they explain it to Mr. Donlevy?

They had to lean against each other to control the laughter.

Long after the laughter, at the end of the day, they sat outside in the schoolyard. The sun warmed their bodies but there was a ripe chill in the air.

"We could've asked him to wait longer," Chad said, his back pressed against the base of the monkey bars, his eyes closed.

Paul, beside him, held his hand up against his eyes. "What're you talking about?"

"Your dad. When we...okay, when *I* was looking for the key. I mean..." Chad opened his eyes. "...your dad is friendly. If we had made up something and told him we needed a little more time, you could've asked him to wait. Then..." He stopped when he saw how hostile Paul looked.

"And exactly what do you think we should've made up? That Beso had peed on the rug and we needed to clean it?"

"Yeah, sure..." Chad looked embarrassed. "I don't know..."

What really got to Paul was how Chad thought Mr. Brager was a real push-over, wimpy compared to how tough his own dad was. Chad would never say it but Paul knew he was thinking it.

"Okay, so maybe I'm wrong. Maybe I do get too curious." When Paul said nothing, still simmering, Chad said, "So tell me about the story." When Paul appeared confused, he added, "The one your dad tells Adrian before he goes to sleep."

"Oh...Oh." Paul perked up and became more animated. "Oh, this is strange."

"Go on."

"Well I told you how my dad likes to tell stories of Norse mythology." Chad nodded. "There's this one he tells a lot about...Well, about Iduna's apples."

"I-doo-naaa?"

Paul laughed out loud. "You sound just like Adrian."

"Oh jeez..."

"Anyway..." Paul looked up at the sky. "It's kinda strange. When Dad first told the story to Adrian, Adrian said he'd never heard it before."

"So?"

"Well you know Adrian. He's kinda a baby sometimes. I think Dad sucks him up and Adrian really goes for it and takes advantage of Dad." Chad waited. "I thought that Adrian was lying, saying he'd never heard it..."

"So has he?"

"Well...Then I got thinking. Maybe Adrian was tellin' the truth...Maybe he really hadn't heard it before." Paul studied Chad's questioning face. "I think that the reason I thought Adrian had heard it before was because...Well, because *I* had heard it before..."

"Where?"

"From Dad. When Adrian was really young and didn't even understand those stories. He just kinda looked at Dad like a...retard..." Paul didn't like using the word but thought Chad might get a chuckle out of it. Chad was quiet. "Just lookin' at Dad with a dumb smile, babbling like a baby. Listenin' to Dad's voice. But, you know, whenever Dad tells it now, I really remember it."

"So what's so special about it?"

"It means something now. I think Dad's tellin' it to get a message across but I don't know exactly what it is. It's about Iduna's apples."

"Who's I-doo-naaaaaa?" Chad wailed. "You're as bad as Arif, keepin' me in suspense."

"Okay, okay." Paul took a breath. "In Norse mythology, Iduna was a goddess who..." And he told the tale about Iduna, the trickery of Loki, and the great flapping monster from the sky.

"And you saw the story again? In that book at Mr. Donlevy's?"

Paul nodded.

"So why's it so spooky? Why'd it get to you?"

Paul sighed.

"Come on, Brager!"

"It's going to sound weird...Like I'm trying to be a detective...That I'm making things up to be creative." He knew that Chad was spellbound. "I didn't get the connections when I was younger and Dad was telling me the story but now...When he tells it to Adrian, I understand completely."

"Understand what, dude?"

"I told my dad that Iduna...That Iduna is my mother... Ida...Get it? Iduna...Ida..." He saw Chad's scrunched-up face, his look of bewilderment. But before he could utter one word, Paul cut in quickly. "I didn't know a thing about the myth until I read the story at Mr. Donlevy's condo...I figured my dad was telling a real myth...If you can call a myth real, that is...I just thought he had made up the names. You know, Iduna...to sound like...Well, to sound like Mom's name. But then...I saw that he hadn't made up any of it."

For a long time, Chad said nothing. Then, "You think your mom's Iduna? She's not even real, Brager."

"There's something else." He swallowed.

"Unh-huh...Go on."

"In the myth..." He licked his lips; his throat felt dry. "...Iduna is married to Bragi, the god of poetry."

"Brager?"

"Bragi...who loved to tell stories. Long, long stories..."

"Brager?"

"Bragi! Man, you're stupid, sometimes."

"Oh, okay. Bragi – Brager. Brager – Bragi. Your parents are gods is what you're sayin'."

"I don't know what I'm sayin'. But think about it. Do you think my dad's trying to tell me something?"

Chad looked away. "Isn't it just a big coincidence? Wait..." Chad was suddenly frozen, his eyes gaping.

"What? What, Chad?"

"What's the name of the big, flapping giant again?"

"Uh...Thee...Thiassi."

Chad's eyes widened. "The one who grabs your mother?"

"Thiassi!"

Chad gulped noticeably. "He wanted apples, Brager. He wanted apples. We both know someone who loves apples. And who wears an eagle ring."

They stared at each other intensely and then simultaneously blurted the name they were both thinking: "Theisen!"

Paul's heart was thumping. He was sure the playground was quaking from the noise. "No wonder he's so interested in me...He wants to...Oh man, he wants to find the treasure...The apples!"

"Yeah, so?"

"I think...Well...Maybe my dad really does know what the *apples* are."

Chad touched his arm and he jumped. "But what are the apples, man? Not those ones he has on his desk. What are the apples?"

"Well I think they're more than just rubies, Chad."

"Rubies are no slouch."

Paul shook his head. "They are when you compare them to eternal life."

The first really big snowfall of the school year came and the kids were having a ball during recess.

A few of Paul's classmates were playing Manhunter and Arif had chosen to be the one to hide. They knew from past experiences he was good at hiding. And running, too.

Paul had split off from the others and had rounded a corner of the school when he saw Liz Parkinson looking puny against the side of the school, her hair picking up tiny flecks of white. She never wore a hat and Paul felt a sudden urge to take off his own, thinking he probably looked like an idiot to her, wearing it, showing he was vulnerable to the elements.

But she appeared to have other things on her mind, looking vulnerable herself, like a little old woman about to collapse.

Paul wasn't sure if he should approach her. She didn't look as if she wanted company right then but then she noticed him and held up a hand in a weak greeting.

He came over and nodded in a burly way, then decided he shouldn't try to appear so tough. Not knowing what to say, he offered, "You didn't find him yet?"

She shook her head.

He was surprised that Elizabeth Bronson wasn't there, stuck to her side as if the snow had frozen them at the waist. Maybe they had had a fight. Maybe that was the reason she was looking miserable.

Paul stood beside her, saying nothing, hoping that just by standing there he could give her some comfort.

Finally, she said, "Do you ever notice that nobody uses the washroom any more? During recess, I mean?"

It was such a strange question that Paul would have started laughing if it wasn't for her complete seriousness.

"Right now I really have to go bad."

This was bizarre. He expected her to spring the joke on him at any moment, knowing she had suckered him into believing she was upset. But she kept that serious expression on her face.

"So go. Take a partner and go. What's stopping you?"

It was strange that he was being the reasonable one. To Liz, of all people.

"No one will go with me." When she saw his puzzled look, she added, "Everyone's *scared* to go in. I guess I could go by myself."

Paul didn't need to ask why they were scared. Even though there was always a teacher on basement duty (Dorian Heights was one of the oldest schools in Toronto and actually had a basement, complete with uneven, cement floors and exposed heating ducts high up on the ceiling), the teacher would never question why a student needed to use the washroom.

However, it happened to be Mr. Theisen who did basement duty all the time now. Or so they thought. Paul was usually having so much fun during recess that, like so many others, he would hold his pee until they had entered the classroom. Then he'd ask Mr. Donlevy if he could go afterwards. Mr. Donlevy wasn't impressed. Paul and the others who postponed using the washroom always answered Mr. Donlevy's questions with, "Well we didn't have to go then."

So, therefore, Paul was never a witness to Mr. Theisen's basement behaviour. It was enough that the basement was already eerie in itself. One could enter it through three, different doors. The doors were all the ends of the letter T and there was a long, dimly-lit corridor going from one door to the next. This meant, of course, that someone might possibly have to turn around a corner, depending on the door he entered and how far away it was from the bathroom.

The rooms in the basement were used as lunchrooms or for the daycare children who occupied them at the end of the school day. The gym was located off to the side but Mr. Rhodes, the much-loved gym teacher, was never in his office during recess so he was never around to bring some relief to those nervous students who came into the basement.

Paul had heard from his fellow classmates that Mr. Theisen seemed to relish scaring the students who came inside. He didn't hide and jump out at them. Nothing like that. He'd just...show up. One moment there'd be nobody in the corridor and one would turn his back for a second, then he'd be there. Or one would come into a long, dark hallway that was completely empty and silent. And then hear his black, polished shoes clicking slowly way down at the end of another hallway.

Kids found it exciting at first, as if Theisen had devised a game especially for them, to match wits or challenge moves of intelligence. But it soon started to make all of them a little creeped-out.

He needed to say nothing, Mr. Theisen. They couldn't really say he was being abusive or unprofessional. What could they say? That he was patrolling the corridor in satanic shoes? He never told the students to get out. He never yelled or spied on anyone. He never even had to enter a washroom to discipline rowdy students. His presence, their knowing he was there, caused everyone to behave.

"I'll go with you," Paul told Liz and his stomach lurched.

She blinked at him. "Are you crazy? You can't come in to the washroom with me!"

But she was grinning and that was something. It gave Paul extra confidence to pursue this concern. At least she was brightening and that was an improvement from when he had first found her, looking sad and small.

"No, no," Paul laughed. "I'll go inside with you. I'll wait in the hall."

"And what will you say to him?"

Paul shrugged although he was beginning to dread that moment. He tried to steady his voice. "I'll tell him the truth." Liz watched him with wide, expectant eyes. "That no one would come with you and you really had to go badly."

She giggled. "Sure. Make me look like a goof!"

"There's nothing wrong with that...Would you rather stay here in pain?"

It didn't take her long to decide. "No. Let's go."

Once inside the school, they noticed the silence and the uneasiness that floated around them. They could still hear the muffled cries of the students playing joyfully outside, a reminder that there was a whole different world from the one they were in right now. But the noise got less as they walked forward.

Mr. Theisen was nowhere to be seen. Nor were there any other students.

Paul could feel Liz bristling beside him. He would not have been alarmed at all if she had reached out and taken his hand. The feeling he had at that moment, the fear of confronting Mr. Theisen along with the excitement of sharing this adventure with Liz, was...*intoxicating*. Mr. Donlevy had taken that word out of one of the short stories the students had read in class and had asked them to find the dictionary definition.

Intoxicating, Paul remembered. *Exciting beyond self-control.* He imagined that *intoxicating* was the way he felt right now. He liked the way the word felt in his mouth, the way it made this situation so clear. He almost said it aloud.

There was another feeling though. Something like betrayal. For this was the first time he knew that Chad was not his sidekick in some strange event.

As they got close to the corner where they'd have to turn to go towards the girls' washroom, Liz stopped.

"He'll be waiting right around that corner," she whispered. "That's his style."

Paul looked at her profile, noticing for the first time how the bridge of her nose had a sharp edge to it. The snow had already turned wet in her hair. He wondered if she noticed things about him.

"Come on," he gurgled back in his throat. He almost did take her hand but then thought again about it because he'd probably end up looking dumb.

They took a collective breath, then rounded the corner, thinking of night-time fears and bad dreams, and...

No one was there.

"Go quickly," Paul said and she peeled off like a child who has just learned to run.

He must be at the other end, Paul thought. Down where the boys' washroom was. This was the wrong thing to be thinking about because it drew attention to the fact that his own bladder was full.

Would Liz wait for him while he used the washroom? he wondered. Then, he let the idea go. He didn't want to look like a chicken.

From what seemed like a vast distance, he heard a footfall. Very faint but approaching. Yes, yes, it was down by the boys' washroom. *Come on Liz, come on*, he thought, ignoring the fact that it usually took girls longer to use the washroom. At least he washed his hands. Most of his friends didn't even bother.

He had to run these meaningless things through his head in order not to think about...

*Click, click, click...*Louder with each step...*Click, click...*

Come on Liz.

Click, click...

And he didn't even call out, announcing himself. He loved this practice of terrifying everyone with his "haunted house" steps.

The moment Liz opened the door, Paul held his finger to his lips, and gestured towards the exit that was in the opposite direction they had come. She had time to hear the ominous steps before they raced towards the door and ran out. Then, once in the schoolyard, they didn't stop running until they were out on the big soccer field, catching their breath and laughing.

They didn't have time to talk about their ordeal because there were Chad and Elizabeth, eying them with suspicion and asking where they had been.

They just kept laughing while Chad and Elizabeth grew frustrated. Then Elizabeth, turning her head, said, "Look!"

They all looked towards the direction she was pointing.

Theisen had just stepped out of the building, looking sleepy like a bear, waking from hibernation. He looked around him as children jaunted in play, then bent down to pick up some of the feathery snow and let it fall between his fingers. He looked from side to side, then straight out to where they were.

"D'ya think he's looking for us?" gulped Liz.

"Shhh..." Paul said, even though there was really no need to be quiet.

But Theisen didn't seem to be aware of the four of them. He seemed intent on the action going on around him. He watched as four kids engaged in a game of chase, then turned to watch as some other kids played soccer with a tennis ball. When they got a clear look at his face, they could see he was smiling.

This was strange in itself because his smile was never aimed at the antics of children.

But there he was, totally ignored by everyone, looking at one scene of immense joy, then revolving to take in another, then almost twirling in some diabolical dance. His smile got huge.

"Do you think he's gone mad?" said Chad.

The smile was not pleasant. No, he wasn't enjoying the escapades of the students. His grin looked...Well, it looked truly evil.

Then, the bell rang.

An incredible transformation came over Theisen as his smile dissolved and he started ordering kids to go inside.

As they lined up inside, next to the classroom, Chad gave Paul a silly grin. Paul had calmed down and saw Liz gushing something to Elizabeth, probably what had happened in the basement.

"What's wrong with you?" Paul finally asked Chad, who made a point of sticking that grin in Paul's face.

"I was talking to Sylvia as we came up the stairs."

"So?"

"She said that you and Liz went into the basement together...Alone."

Paul reddened. At least it felt like he did. "Yeah...She had to use the washroom."

"So she took you?"

"No girls would go with her."

"So she didn't go by herself? She took you."

Paul ignored him as Mr. Donlevy greeted them and allowed them to enter. This was the first time he didn't feel like sitting next to Chad and his simpering grin.

"Why...?"

"We'll talk about this later, Tremblay."

Before Mr. Donlevy could even get into a lesson, a number of students asked, in almost panic-stricken tones, if they could use the washroom.

Mr. Donlevy put down his chalk and stared at them. "Okay, this is getting way out of hand. Is this a game? A bet you're having with each other?"

Finally, a timid girl named Patricia said, "No, Mr. Donlevy. It's not like we can help it!"

"What do you mean?"

Patricia rarely spoke up so Mr. Donlevy could see the seriousness of the situation.

"It's Mr...Theisen."

"Okay...Go on."

"Well he..."

"He's the Phantom of the Basement," blurted Tony. "He lurks down there to scare us, I swear."

There were a few nervous laughs.

"Yeah, like he's on duty every recess. You and the other teachers used to do basement duty, Mr. Donlevy. What happened?"

Mr. Donlevy nodded, slightly embarrassed. "Yes, we did. But at a staff meeting, Mr. Theisen said he wanted to...be in that area...for a few days."

"A few days? It's been a month now!"

"Why did he need to...be there?" This came from Liz.

"There were some problems...as you all know...Kids standing on toilets, kids running down the halls. Things like that. These got reported to him and he...made the decision to check things out for himself."

"So he didn't think the other teachers could handle it?" asked Arif. He always knew where to hit a nerve.

All their eyes were trained on Mr. Donlevy.

"Well, yes...But it's the principal's job to oversee the teachers, too...So that the school can function smoothly." It was a perfectly reasonable answer though Mr. Donlevy seemed doubtful about his own words.

"Well couldn't Mrs. Tarnapulsky do the duty? She's the vice-principal..."

"...and *she* wouldn't scare us," someone finished the sentence.

Paul sensed a revolt about to happen around him. People were really bothered.

"You think he tries to scare you on purpose?" asked Mr. Donlevy.

A number of heads nodded at each other.

"Does he say things to you?"

"No. He just walks around like a zombie. He just looks at you...with those eyes."

"The bathrooms seemed okay last year," Elizabeth said boldly. "When Mr. Myers was here." This received a chorus of cheers and agreements.

Paul didn't think Mr. Donlevy was in the mood to defend Mr. Theisen but he probably felt he had to do something. "Okay, okay...I think Mr. Theisen is just trying to do his job...I really believe he's not trying to scare you... On purpose, anyway."

All of them in that classroom really wanted Mr. Donlevy to bash Mr. Theisen somehow, to let go of his civility and criticize Theisen in front of them. They also knew this wouldn't happen because teachers always stand up for each other, no matter what. But we do it, too, Paul thought.

"Maybe he's not trying to do it on purpose," said Vafa and the room went silent. "But kids are still getting scared. Mr. Donlevy, if kids in grade seven are freaking out, imagine how the grade ones feel. At least we can... Well, wait to use the washroom."

"Yeah," said Tony, "those guys would pee themselves."

"Are you saying," Mr. Donlevy began, "that that's why you're not using the washroom?"

"That's what we're telling you," Rodrigo said. "That's why this is an emergency."

And then a really weird thing happened. Mr. Donlevy agreed to take the entire class into the hallway and down to the washrooms. And, as if every single teacher on that floor had had the exact same conversation with their class that Mr. Donlevy had had with his, all doors opened at the same time, and there was a parade of students in the hall, flocking towards the washrooms.

Paul remembered Mr. Donlevy and the other teachers exchanging odd looks. At one point, Mr. Donlevy passed Mrs. Middleton and said, "We've got a major crisis here," and Mrs. Middleton, her eyes troubled, nodded.

As things went, they got settled again and into the lesson. Mr. Donlevy promised he would talk to Mr. Theisen and they believed him, although they didn't envy him the task.

After school, Mr. Donlevy took Paul and Chad aside. They thought he was going to say something about Mr. Theisen, perhaps that he really was a robot or a clone. It turned out the topic was completely different.

"I'm going away for Christmas," he said, and when Paul and Chad didn't respond, he added, "Surprise, surprise."

"Where you going this time?"

"England."

"Wowww..."

"Do you have relatives there, Mr. Donlevy?"

"No."

It always amazed them that he could just pack up and go to places where nobody knew him and where he was a complete stranger. Once, he had even told them, sometimes he felt more comfortable being around people he didn't know, being around people who didn't know his history.

"Anyway, I have a similar situation to the one at Thanksgiving. Concerning Beso, I mean. Mom," he said and the word sounded strange coming out of his mouth, "will take Beso for the holidays but she can't take him the last Friday of school."

"Ummm..." said Chad and both Mr. Donlevy and Paul looked at him. He was looking a little pale. "Uh...I don't think I'd be able to come this time, Mr. Donlevy. I...uh...My relatives are visiting that night." But there was something false about his words. Paul had known him long enough to detect a lie. And it would've had to have been a big lie for Chad to avoid Beso's company.

Mr. Donlevy looked at Paul.

"Uh," he said, feeling Chad's body stiffen beside him. "I don't think my family's doing anything special that night. I'd have to check."

"Of course." Mr. Donlevy looked at Chad. "That's too bad. Perhaps another time." Then he looked back at Paul. "But not alone, right. If you can do it, you don't come alone."

Paul nodded. "I'd need someone to drive me anyway."

As Paul walked away with Chad, it was the second time in one day that he felt he had betrayed him.

Chapter 7: Mr. Donlevy's Journals

Paul felt horrible.

He had lied to his dad. And he had done so in such a convincing way that Mr. Brager's expression indicated he believed Paul.

Mr. Brager had consented that Paul take care of Beso after school.

But this time, Paul was going to leave for the condo without Chad. This, Mr. Brager did not know. Paul had told him that Mr. Tremblay was picking Chad and him up from school and driving them to the condo. Paul hated including Chad in the lie since Chad, his best friend, was completely innocent in the devious plot. He also hated using Mr. Tremblay who he suspected was the reason behind Chad's not coming in the first place. And, Paul figured, even if Chad were part of a lie, Mr. Tremblay would still find an excuse for blaming him.

Paul had never lied to his father before so there was really no reason for his dad to question him.

Paul squirmed a lot though, imagining every dire thing that could possibly happen. The worst obviously being that he got abducted on the subway as he travelled to the condo. Being dead wasn't what scared him. His real fear was having his dad discover the truth. Or, what if he met one of his dad's colleagues on the subway? (Mr. Brager worked for *The Toronto Star* and often spoke of some of the employees working the night shift in order to get the paper out in the morning).

Paul said that he would eat supper at Chad's house after he took Beso for his first walk and then stay at Chad's place until the evening when they'd go back for Beso's second walk which was the late one.

So, really, Paul's dad didn't expect him to walk through the front door until ten o'clock or even later.

Mr. Brager was okay with this but kept asking if the Tremblays were okay with all the fuss, giving Paul supper and such. Paul assured him everything was okay and Mr. Brager said they'd have to do the same for Chad one day.

Like they hadn't many times before, Paul thought.

Of course there were holes in his story but he had time to patch them up before he saw his dad next.

He also had to lie to Chad. Before Chad went home, he wished Paul a *Merry Christmas!* and told him to hug Beso for him. When he asked Paul if his dad were picking him up from the school, Paul said, yes, he'd be there shortly.

Chad said, "We'll have a good year, buddy! You *will* promise me one thing, right?"

"Sure," Paul said, hesitantly.

"You find that key! But don't open the desk until I'm there with you. Deal?"

"Deal," Paul said and they touched knuckles.

Then, Chad was off and Paul was alone. More alone than he'd ever felt.

Paul drew up his coat and put on his toque. His knapsack was pressed against his back and seemed to be prodding him about the big mistake he was making. Oh well, he told himself, too late to change things now.

He had a good idea as to how to reach the condo by streetcar and subway. Mr. Donlevy had explained the journey to Chad and him once when they had asked him if he owned a car.

The trip went without any problems. In fact, he felt invigorated that his independence was getting stronger. He was getting more comfortable doing things like this and talking to Liz.

He did wish for Chad's company. Not because he was nervous but because he needed the silly banter they often engaged in.

The wind was whipping up steadily as Chris permitted him into the building.

"Your friend not with you this time?"

"No. He had to go visit some relatives." Then he told Chris that his dad was waiting for him outside.

"Tell him he can park in visitors' parking. There's some space left. It'll probably get busy soon. You know. Holiday guests."

"No, that's okay. He found parking. He's doing some last-minute shopping."

Jeez, he thought, once you got into this lying thing, it started to get easy.

Again, Beso barked before he entered. He jumped up, letting Paul cradle his head in his hands. Mr. Donlevy had told them that he had had Beso cut at the end of October so that he'd have his warm fur back for the cold weather. This time, Paul could actually see Beso's eyes without having to smooth his hair back.

Being there, having Beso's sudden company, put Paul in good spirits.

When they came back in from the walk and Paul had fed Beso, he decided to phone his dad. He hadn't asked

Paul to but it made Paul feel better. Besides, it was his sneaky way of finding out if his dad had stumbled onto his plan.

"Hey, what's up?"

There was no edge or suspicion to his dad's voice so Paul figured that his plan was still intact. He had had no concern that Chad would phone his house, knowing Paul was at the condo anyway. Besides, Chad usually contacted him on his cellphone.

"Hi. I just wanted to say that we're at the condo... Everything's fine." He was impressed at the steadiness in his voice.

"Oh. Thanks for calling. Then you're going back to Chad's, right?"

"Right."

"Catch you later."

With just a tinge of guilt in him, Paul ended the call. Beso finished his food and looked up at him. Even *his* look seemed to be accusing Paul of treachery. Paul checked out the contents in Mr. Donlevy's fridge. He had plenty of time before searching for the desk key.

Paul took out a can of coke and a couple of wedges of cheese, reminding himself he had to consider his food intake and his energy level. Supper would have to be improvised. He flicked stations on television as he lounged in an armchair, chewing, drinking, burping, and generally feeling like a slob. Sitting there, he looked around the living-room. It was like having his own apartment and no one, not even Adrian, could penetrate his private existence.

He could have sat there longer, enjoying his new freedom, but he had a job to do and he was getting anxious. He went to the computer room, Beso right at his heels. "Man, if you could talk," he said and Beso wagged his tail.

Paul spent a lot of time going through the books that Chad hadn't had time to reach. There were periods when he asked himself why he was doing this at all, why it really did matter as to what he might find. What exactly did he *want* to find? And if he did find something really strange, would it change his perception of Mr. Donlevy? Their relationship? What if there were something illegal in there? Something that would force him to inform the police?

He stopped taking out books. He hadn't even thought about this last possibility. For if he did have to contact the police, his dad and Chad and everyone else would learn that he had been snooping through Mr. Donlevy's condo... alone. And that he had gone to the condo...alone.

But his curiosity wouldn't allow him any more time to think about these things. Mechanically, without any kind of regret, his brain ordered his hands to start working on the books again.

His heartbeat sped up a little when he reached the Poe biographies and the collections of Poe's literature. He remembered that Poe was Mr. Donlevy's favourite author. And if one's going to hide a key in a book, why not in one by his favourite author?

No luck.

No luck with any of the books.

He was discouraged. He looked at his watch: seven o'clock. He had wasted an hour and, for all he knew, the key might not have been in the condo at all. It could have been dangling from a key chain that was now somewhere in England. And if it were here, it could have been in hundreds of places.

He jumped up and tried the drawers again, a faint hope that Mr. Donlevy had left them unlocked this time.

He hadn't.

A new feeling came over him. If he found the key and opened the drawers, what if he was to find nothing interesting? What if he found old war medallions, or something he cared nothing about?

He sat down and Beso curled up beside him. He glanced around. If the key were in the condo, it must be in this very room, he told himself. Why would Mr. Donlevy go to the trouble of hiding it elsewhere? Or try to hide it at all? The security in the building was excellent. Did he think someone could even get up to his penthouse past security, break through his lock and alarm system, and search around for a key, not even knowing one existed?

Or perhaps? Was he purposely hiding something from just Chad and him?

"It has to be in this room," he informed Beso whose little stub of a tail shook violently.

He started looking around the computer, behind the monitor, and other places. Then, he opened a small, blue CD-ROM-holder.

And there it was! Or, at least, there was a key.

How stupid he and Chad had been, so concerned about mystery and intrigue and silly movie plots that they had wasted all that time on the books. He had heard many times before that the things people cannot find are often in the most obvious of places.

He studied his hand as he picked out the key. He was actually shaking. What if it's not even the right key? Wouldn't that be ridiculous?

He could feel his heart thudding as he made his way to the desk.

There was a little ding as the key connected with something in the first lock. He took it back out and slowly opened the drawer.

Duotangs. Only duotangs.

He lifted up about five of them, all thick with three-holed paper, and looked under them to see if there was something more satisfying.

Nothing.

He closed the drawer angrily, reminding himself afterwards to be gentle.

He opened the other drawers. They contained duotangs also. And under each pile, absolutely nothing valuable or mysterious.

He sat in frustration. War medallions would've been more interesting. Instead, he had only found Mr. Donlevy's old teaching notes. All his old, boring...

Or were they?

Each duotang had dates written on the front which was Paul's reason for believing they contained teaching notes from those years listed. But when he brought them up closer to his eye, there was a word pencilled in above the dates. And the word was...

Journal.

A journal? Liz Parkinson had told him once that she had her own personal journal. And Mr. Donlevy himself had distributed notebooks to them at the beginning of September and told them that these would be their journals. That they'd be writing in them about their own thoughts, ideas, maybe even secrets, twice a week. And that if they wrote something so personal that they didn't want him to read, they should let him know.

So these were Mr. Donlevy's own personal journals. Paul turned one over in his hands. Then, he looked more steadily at the dates. The dates must have been the time lines for each particular journal. And after some research, he learned that the earliest one went back about ten years.

Or were they journals? Perhaps Mr. Donlevy had labelled them as journals to disguise something else.

He opened one, began to read it, then closed it quickly.

Yep. Definitely journals.

He wondered if there was anything written about the students in there.

For a long time, he thought about reading from a journal or two. Then, he forced himself to put the journals back and lock up the drawers.

Reading them would have been wrong: a violation of privacy. He couldn't go that far. But then he laughed to himself. Who was he kidding? If these had been Liz Parkinson's journals, he would already be half-way through the first one by now.

He was now glad that Chad wasn't there. Chad would have encouraged him to read the journals along with him and he knew he would not have said no.

He was careful about leaving the room exactly as he had found it. The key was back in its home. He shut the door, proud of his self-restraint.

Looking at his watch, he noticed that it was around seven thirty. He had a decision to make.

He couldn't stay in the condo until Beso's next walk because Chris would probably get suspicious as to why he would be up there all night while his dad was shopping.

He decided to go downstairs and go out and find a cheap restaurant. Maybe there was a McDonald's nearby. He didn't have too much money.

But he still had to drop off the key.

Luckily, Chris was talking to someone else so he didn't have time to say much to Paul. He did ask if everything was okay and he looked at Paul as if he could detect something strange was going on. Paul produced a big smile and said his dad had called him on his cell and was meeting him outside. He rushed off before Chris could ask any questions about why he'd been so long upstairs.

The snow was falling in big, wet chunks. Although he was excited about Christmas, he was nervous about this odd night. Walking aimlessly in a part of the city he did not know. Thinking about his next move.

He didn't feel much like eating at McDonald's by himself. He also didn't want to have to deal with Chris again, lying to him that, oh yes, his dad was waiting for him outside and, oh no, he didn't want to come in and sit in the lobby.

Chris wasn't stupid.

So he made a quick decision.

When he walked in the front door of his house at almost eight thirty, Adrian came bounding over, not even giving him a chance to take off his snowy boots. "Yo, Paul! Hey, aren't you supposed...?"

"Chad's not feeling well," he said, shoving Adrian aside and speaking directly to his dad. "We thought it was a good idea for me to come home. Mr. Tremblay drove me here."

"What's wrong with him?" chirped Adrian, always curious.

Paul cast him a look of irritation. "I don't know. It's probably the flu. He's throwing up a lot."

"Ewwww!"

Paul saw the horrific look on his dad's face. "They don't think it's serious. They think he just needs lots of sleep."

"Poor guy. And so close to Christmas."

Paul's mind was swirling. He had to keep running things through his head so that he didn't end up contradicting his own lies, so that he could prepare for any questions that might be thrown at him.

And he didn't like the way his dad was looking at him now, almost amused. "I hope you don't catch it. Whatever he has."

"Yeah!" belted out Adrian. "Then all of us get sick and...Man, I don't wanna be sick for Christmas! Stay away from us, Paul!" And he held up two fingers to form a cross.

"I didn't see Mr. Tremblay's car outside."

"No," Paul said, avoiding his father's eyes. "I told him he could let me off at the end of the street."

"That was generous of you. Are the roads slippery?"

"A little."

"But you have to go and walk Beso one more time, right? Will Mr. Tremblay...?"

"Well, actually...I was going to ask..."

"Of course," Mr. Brager answered, "I can take you."

"All right!" yelled Adrian. "I finally get to see Beso!" And he slammed a fist into an open palm.

Chapter 8: The Dream

Things were not right with Mr. Donlevy in the beginning of the new year and they all noticed it.

Paul thought at first it had something to do with his finding the journals, that he had somehow left evidence that he had rummaged around in Mr. Donlevy's personal belongings and Mr. Donlevy knew about it.

There were a couple of times when Paul argued with himself about approaching him and admitting the crime. He'd assure Mr. Donlevy that he read nothing, absolutely nothing.

He didn't though because he could see something of a much more sinister nature was bothering Mr. Donlevy.

He tried to deliver his lessons with the passion he always had but they, at times, fell flat and lifeless.

The students were polite. They showed patience, hoping that whatever was bothering him would be gone by the next day.

During one recess, they discussed the situation.

"Maybe he's just depressed about coming back from his trip," said Michael. "You know how much he loves to travel. He even told us that time that if he had enough money, he'd stop teaching and travel for the rest of his life."

"Yeah, but he wasn't depressed after Thanksgiving," Chad pointed out.

"Maybe there was a tragedy in his family. Maybe his mom or dad died," offered Liz.

"I don't even think he has a dad," Chad said, then looked nervous as if he had said too much. He glanced at Paul but no one even took an interest in the dad thing.

"Or Beso," said Rodrigo who had taken a keen interest in the dog ever since he had translated Beso's name into English for everyone. "Maybe something happened to Beso."

They all looked unhappy. After all, they had more of a connection with Beso than they had with Mr. Donlevy's parents.

Chad drew Paul aside. "Did Beso seem okay when you saw him last?"

"Yeah, but remember, it was only the beginning of the Christmas break when I saw him."

"Do you think one of us should ask him?" Vafa said.

"I think maybe we should let it go for a few days. Maybe he'll be...well...happy again after this week. Plus, maybe he's not ready to talk about it." This came from Liz.

"Well, you know, people don't always have to be smiling and cute to be happy," Paul said, thinking of the clownish smiles of certain adults they knew.

Liz looked at him. "Do you get the idea that he's happy, Paul?"

He looked down. "Well no, I guess not."

"Yo, yo, what's the talk?"

Arif was there. No, he wouldn't miss this for a second.

"We're talking about why Mr. Donlevy is so upset."

"So you know?"

They moved in closer.

"You don't know?"

They looked at him, their eyes wide and waiting.

"It may have somethin' to do with why he's upset."

"Come on Arif, recess is almost over."

He smiled a big, wide smile. An Arif smile. The bait for the worm. Worms. "You know Peter Stavros? He's in Mrs. Middleton's class."

They all knew him and they all knew he and Arif were close. They nodded.

"Well he was telling me that he came in extra early this morning. Like around eight. His dad had to go in early for work and dropped off Pete. Well Pete wandered around the halls until Mrs. Turner got on his case and told him to go to the office, seeing there was no teacher on duty yet."

"Go on, Khaled. Get to the goods."

"Anyway, he was sittin' in the office, gettin' real bored, watchin' the teachers come in to sign in and check their mailboxes..." He loved drawing this out, they could tell. "Mr. Donlevy came in and said *Hi* to Pete...Pete said he seemed fine. You know, the old Mr. Donlevy...But then... For some reason, Mr. Ghoul..." They had come to know that this was Arif's name for their new principal. "He came out of his office as if he could see through walls...He and Donlevy stared at each other like...well, Pete says, like two boxers about to go at it...He told Donlevy to come into the office and Donlevy went right in. As if he'd been expecting it. Pete said he didn't show any surprise."

"And?"

"Pete said things got real weird in the office. Everyone seemed nervous. Anyway, Mr. Donlevy wasn't there for a real long time but when he came out..."

They all leaned in even closer. Paul could feel Liz's breath, warm on his cheek.

"He had turned into a vampire?" joked Tony.

"He was so mad, man. Just by looking at his face, Pete could tell Mr. Theisen..." It had been the first time Arif had used the principal's actual name and they all looked at each other as if he had suddenly changed the topic. "... had said something that really got him going."

They all moved back – like a huge flower, once strangled by lack of sunlight, now blossoming in the frigid schoolyard.

"Then Mrs. Franklin told Pete it was eight thirty and he could go outside now."

"What do you think...Ghoul...said?"

"Well it couldn't have been about a phone call for Mr. Donlevy...Telling him about a family emergency, I mean... Mr. Donlevy wouldn't have come back to class," said Vafa in a rational tone.

"Maybe he's going to get transferred," Sylvia said, "like Mr. Myers."

"Maybe he's fired."

"Maybe it doesn't even have anything to do with school...Maybe Mr. Theisen just told a really bad joke and Mr. Donlevy got offended."

They all stared at Tony until he lost himself in laughter.

"I'm a little upset," said Chad. "I mean, where does this guy get his power? Taking it out on kids is one thing but...teachers? And good teachers...I don't care about the crappy ones...He has to be stopped."

This was the most passionate Paul had ever seen Chad and he wondered if there was more to this than just Chad's concern for Mr. Donlevy.

"Maybe we should report him!"

People were looking oddly at Chad.

Arif broke out with a laugh. "And say what, Tremblay? He stared at us? Hypnotized us with his eyes?"

Now everyone was laughing, even Chad. Tony looked envious but grinned nonetheless.

"I mean, we don't exactly have much to go on."

"No real evidence," threw in Rodrigo.

"Yeah, you stop him, Tremblay. You just try to. Yeah, you de man!"

The bell rang shortly after and they went inside.

Mr. Donlevy was still troubled. In fact, there were times when he got angry at them. Anger from a teacher was not unusual. But anger over tiny things was.

There were a couple of times when someone would get out of his seat to sharpen his pencil and Mr. Donlevy would demand that he sit down, that he was disrupting the lesson and that this kind of behaviour was unacceptable.

They wouldn't have been surprised if Mrs. Middleton was telling them this, but not Mr. Donlevy. Something was really rattling him.

He did manage to apologize to them at the end of the day. He said he'd had a really bad day and he shouldn't have taken his frustration out on the class. That was wrong. It wasn't their fault. At one point, he almost seemed about to cry.

They didn't ask any questions. They figured he would eventually open up to them. They could only look at him and feel sorry for him and for something they didn't understand.

The plane was going down and there was nothing they could do about it.

He was just a kid so he was not surprised that he wasn't feeling heroic. But there were tons of adults on that plane, some of whom were big, football-size guys, their arms thick and meaty, and even they were squealing and rushing around like he was.

The screams were girly and high-pitched and he really wanted to save everyone. You know. Dash into the cockpit and grab the steering mechanism and jerk them up away from the dull blue of the water beneath them. To let everyone know he was in control and, even though he was only twelve, he could still land them safely. He really wanted to grin at all those beefy men and see them look down, ashamed.

But he couldn't.

Whatever the pilot and co-pilot were doing, it wasn't stopping the water below from coming up, up, closer, closer, towards them. They could see it through the windows and they knew they were doomed. They knew life was over. But there was another feeling beyond this fear: the helplessness of not being able to do anything to save themselves.

Then, for the first time, he became aware of his father beside him. But he wasn't looking at Paul. He had this terrible look of concern on his face as he looked down at the bundle in his arms. Drawing aside part of the sheet wrapped around the bundle to get a look at what was under the sheet.

He looked hard at his dad's face, not remembering the lines of age grooved into his forehead, the droopy bags under his eyes, the frosted hair about to break off like icicles. The total look of despair in lost eyes. As he looked at the bundle.

And the bundle was Adrian.

Tiny and babyish. Shrunken, deformed. Face lifeless and white. Drained.

Then, startling him, his dad glanced over. "He's dying," he mouthed, the words caught back in his throat. "He's dying."

For a second, Adrian's eyes flickered open. Understanding. Looking wiser than Paul had ever seen him. Then, his eyes closed again.

His dad was looking at him, open-mouthed.

They on the plane had stopped screaming at the same time even though they were plunging at mind-blowing speed. And their sudden silence caused total calm among everyone.

Their head swivelled as if connected in the same machine and they looked towards the front. Something there was compelling them to look.

A huge man, his long hair curling down onto his shoulders, his beard so full that it reached an immense width. His hand, fleshy and etched with wormy veins, came up to calm them even more. It was so big, it could've enveloped Paul's head with one squeeze. But, in no way, was his presence frightening.

Was it an angel of some kind?

It didn't have wings but there was definitely a body. A body that was bright white and flashing. He couldn't tell if it wore clothes because the light was so blinding. They all had to cover their eyes.

Even when it spoke, telling them it was there to save them, its voice was a mystery. Bubbly but rich in tone. "Don't panic," it told them, "you are safe with me. Have no fear. My name is..."

But Paul could not make out the name. Over-something.

"You won't let the plane crash?" Paul asked, feeling soothed all of a sudden.

It looked at him, saying nothing.

But then an even stranger thing happened. Everyone started screaming again. That is, everyone except for Paul and his dad and brother. Paul and his father glanced

*at each other with these stupidly serene grins. As if they
knew they were going to be okay.*

"Paul," the angel said.

*He looked back at it and repeated the question, "You
won't let the plane crash?"*

And, again, it said his name.

Then its face twisted into his father's and he was
there, gently shaking his shoulder. "Paul...Paul..."

Paul sat up in his bed, his eyes wide. "Wow," he said,
"that was so real."

"Are you okay?"

"Yeah...Yeah..." He blinked and looked around. He saw
the safe, familiar surroundings of his bedroom. "I just had
this really weird dream."

"I know. You were talking in your sleep."

Paul blinked at him, embarrassed.

"Sure you're okay?"

"Yeah, why?"

"Adrian's not."

Paul arched his neck to look below him. He saw
Adrian's sheets all bunched-up and wet-looking. Adrian
was not there. Paul remembered the dream and panicked.
"What's wrong?"

"Calm down, calm down. He's okay. Just a little
sick."

Paul looked at Adrian's sheets again. "Did he...? I
mean, I didn't even hear him."

"You must've been so wrapped up in your dream. He
woke me up with his howling."

Paul imagined his brother turning into a werewolf, his
canine teeth sharpening, his fat cheeks sprouting hair. It
would have been laughable if not for the strange day Paul
was beginning to have. "Where is he?"

"I've got him at the kitchen table. He has a fever." Mr. Brager pointed to Adrian's sheets. "That's sweat. It's not what you think."

Paul kicked his feet over the side of the bed and jumped down hard to the floor, trying to avoid touching any of his brother's mess. He was disgusted.

"Listen, I'm going to stay home and keep an eye on him. Do you mind taking the streetcar into school?"

"Not at all." In fact, he would enjoy not having the company of his brother.

"And telling them at the school that Adrian won't be in?"

"Sure, Dad."

After washing up, Paul went out to the kitchen, expecting to see Adrian faking his illness, sniffling and coughing, covering up a mischievous grin when his dad wasn't looking. But what about the bed? he thought. You can't fake sweat.

Adrian had his head down on the table and he was moaning a bit.

Brager pulled up a chair beside him and appeared genuinely concerned. He rubbed Adrian's back. "What can I do, kiddo?"

Paul remained standing, horrified that his brother might spew vomit at him.

"Get some breakfast," his dad said.

"Actually, I'm not very hungry."

His dad looked at him. "Not you, too."

Paul couldn't hold his dad's stare for long. "I'll get some breakfast," he said, thinking, better to get puked on than try to explain things to Dad.

"Dad, am I gonna die?"

"Of course not, Adrian. We all get sick. You'll be fine."

After he had wolfed down his cornflakes, Paul brushed his teeth, got changed, and left for school.

Chad and he gave each other a high-five and before Chad could even say a word, Paul said, "Man, did I have this weird dream last night. Actually, this morning."

"What about?"

Paul told him and then wondered what Chad made of it.

"You say Adrian was sick in the dream?" Paul nodded. "And he really is sick now?" Paul nodded again. "Man, I've heard of this happening before."

"Heard of what happening?"

"Like, you know, when you dream up something and it comes true."

Paul looked doubtful. "Or maybe, in my subconsciousness, I really knew he was lying there sick and then I made that part of my dream. That happens, too."

"True...but...but what does the plane mean? Or that God-thing? Are you goin' on any trips soon?"

Paul shook his head.

"Because that would be just plain freaky."

They started moving together, out towards the middle of the soccer field which had a shiny, hardened, white surface on it now. The walk was treacherous and they had to tread carefully, seeing they had been too obstinate to wear winter boots.

Chad almost fell and caught Paul's coat sleeve. "Wait a moment! Hey, Mr. Donlevy likes to travel. Was he on the plane?"

Paul thought back. "No."

"Was Mr. Donlevy the angel-thing?"

"No way. Didn't even look like him. I told you, man. It was huge and had lots of hair and its name was Over-something. It was as if it didn't want me to know its name."

Chad was silent for awhile before saying in an ominous voice, "So didja die?"

"No. I guess the thing saved us."

Chad showed an expression that he was deep in thought. "Over...Over...I wonder what that means. And what about Adrian? You don't think he's gonna die, do you?"

"No. Everyone gets the flu about this time of year."

When the bell sounded for them to go inside, Mr. Theisen was at the doors, planting himself in the middle of the hall, the way he always did, a big, merciless grin stuck to his face. Even his greetings seemed sinister and mocking. The corners of his mouth went up even more when Paul passed and Paul wanted to slug him. Did he know something about Adrian? Paul wondered. Paul glanced at Mr. Theisen's ring as he passed, checking out the twisted wings of the eagle.

Meanwhile, Mr. Donlevy was like the other half of Theisen, looking more pathetic than he ever had. Tired, withdrawn, helpless. Many of them wanted to approach him and to see if they could say something that might cheer him.

At the end of the day, Chad had to leave early and Paul lingered as his classmates slowly left the room.

When Mr. Donlevy saw that he was alone with Paul, he managed a smile and said, "What do you want to know, Paul?"

Paul walked over and sat at a desk near Mr. Donlevy. "Are you sick?"

"No...Well, not physically."

Paul narrowed his look. "It's Theisen, isn't it? We all think that Theisen said something to you to make you upset." His voice was full of scorn.

Mr. Donlevy chuckled. "Guessing at things can get you into trouble." When he saw Paul's expression soften a little, he added, "It's a good guess."

"So what was it, Mr. Donlevy? What did he say?" When Mr. Donlevy did not respond, Paul said, "You can't tell me, can you?"

"Not exactly."

"Are you fired? Tell me that, at least. It's only fair." Paul felt silly afterwards, saying this last part.

"No. I'm not fired."

"Well. Did he insult you?"

Mr. Donlevy put his hand up. "Listen, all I can tell you is...Well, he said something about the school that I totally disagree with...I can't say what...But, you see, I can't tell anyone about it...Not even you."

Paul was puzzled. "Not even the other teachers?"

Mr. Donlevy shook his head. "Not even them."

"Is it blackmail? Is he blackmailing you?"

"Paul, listen, I don't want to get you or anyone else in trouble."

"But is it, Mr. Donlevy? Is it blackmail?"

Mr. Donlevy sighed. "If you must know...Yes...It is a kind of blackmail...Mr. Theisen is a dangerous man and I'm..."

"Can't you get help from the police?"

"I see how passionate you are about this, Paul, but... No, the police won't be able to help...It's beyond that. It would only make the situation worse." He saw Paul's look of futility. "There is someone who I think can help, though."

For some reason, Paul wanted to tell him about the dream. As if it were a piece of the puzzle, a clue to helping Mr. Donlevy. "Well...Who can help you? Who is it?"

"I can't tell you that but..."

"Yes?"

"I think you'll find out soon enough."

Paul steadied his look at him. "Can I help?"

"Just by talking to me, you are helping, Paul. But no more than that. Don't approach Theisen. Stand clear of him. I am devising a plan, believe me."

"You mean...to get rid of him?"

"Perhaps...You're not stupid. I'm not going to lie to you. But Paul, this is between you and me, okay? Don't even tell Chad."

Paul nodded. "Would he do anything to the students? Theisen, I mean."

Mr. Donlevy's face darkened. "I believe he already has."

"Is he...?"

"Paul, trust me, I'm working on it...and I'm getting help."

PART II

Chapter 9: Mr. Theisen Gains Control

Adrian's condition faded in and out during January and February. He often showed good spirits one day, only to collapse in pain and discomfort the next. The inconsistency of his ailment confused his father, who had been taking off more and more time at work.

Even though Paul did not have the affection for his brother that his father had, he didn't like the situation at all. He was especially worried about his father who seemed to be aging quickly. He even offered to stay home with Adrian on the days when Adrian was too weak to attend school. That was the proof that Adrian was not faking anything. He loved school so much, there was no way he would have tried to get out of attending classes. Paul's dad said no, Paul should go to school.

But the situation concerning Adrian was more serious than that.

Paul had noticed that other students had been missing school due to illness. Many teachers and parents rationalized that this was not unusual during flu season but Paul suspected something worse. He hadn't told his father yet about the student absences but he figured he would very soon. He kept thinking about that day in the schoolyard when Theisen was frolicking in the snow like a little kid. He wondered, for some reason, if that were connected to the bout of sicknesses.

One day, Paul came home and found his dad sitting listlessly in an armchair, looking haggard. "Is he okay?" Paul asked.

"I think it's getting worse."

Mr. Brager had taken Adrian to their family doctor a few times, anxious to hear anything about what Adrian might have. And, each time, Dr. Samuels said that he could not understand the cause of the illness. For the first time in his medical career, he said, he had no idea of what his patient was suffering.

Samuels was a professional man, a hard-working man. Dedicated to his job. He always tried to bring the best care to those he attended. And he was honest. Brager knew all these things and so when Samuels seemed genuinely perplexed, Brager knew he wasn't trying to sugar-coat any of the facts.

So Samuels recommended different specialists.

And that's when Brager got really scared, when even they seemed lost for answers.

"Where is he?" Paul asked, throwing his coat over a chair.

"In the bedroom. You still feel okay?"

Paul nodded and sat heavily. "You want me to do anything, Dad?"

His father shook his head. Then, slowly, his head tilted up as he looked at his son. "There's something you should know."

Paul's heartbeat jumped.

"I quit my job today."

"Oh Daaaddd..."

"It's all right. I think I had to...For now, anyway. While I take care of this...They're very good to me at work.

They're giving me a leave of absence. You might say my job's on hold."

Paul sighed more dramatically than he thought. "Can he talk?"

"Yeah, a little...But even that tires him out. If things get worse, I may think about hiring a nurse...He's still eating. And I give him the vitamins. Do you know...?"

"What?"

"How are other kids at the school? Are they...Well... catching anything? Are there any like Adrian?"

"Um...Not that I know." Paul wasn't ready to go into that right now. He was too anxious to discuss another matter. He looked directly at his father, summoning the courage he had wanted for so long. "Dad, I think I know."

"You think you know what?" his dad asked but Paul could see it wasn't really a question his father needed to ask.

"I think I know what's happened to Adrian. And I think you know, too."

His father swallowed hard. "By God, you've gotten wise in a short time."

"Well, come on Dad. Look at you. Look at your hair. Look at your eyes. You're getting older, aren't you? I mean...Getting older fast. Too fast."

His dad looked crestfallen and tried to regain his composure. "Yes. You're right. In fact, I didn't just quit my job for Adrian...I quit it because...I just can't..." He glanced down and held his head in his hands.

Paul walked over and rubbed his dad's arm. It was the way his father had done this so many times with him. "It's the story, isn't it? The one about Bragi and Iduna and..." Paul's throat clicked loudly. "And that creep, Thiassi. Theisen is Thiassi. I know that. And that's why he wears that ring. But I just don't get it."

Brager looked up. "What don'tcha get?"

"Why you? Why us? Why now? Isn't this all...Well, isn't this in the past?"

"The past always comes back, Paul. In some way, in some form. Believe me, until a few months ago, I just thought I was Mr. Fredrik Brager. Widower and father of two boys. Nothing special about me, nothing remotely *historical* about me. But then...Then everything started to come together. When you and Adrian started to talk about Theisen...And he said he knew me...Everything made sense."

"But do you...You know, remember anything? From long ago, I mean?"

"No. It was another time...Right now, I don't even know what to do. How to stop him, I mean."

There was some silence before Paul said, "Do you think we can help Adrian though?" What Paul really meant was, could they help all the students? He suddenly realized they were all in danger.

His father's face clouded over again. "No. I think that Theisen has to be defeated. I think that all things done can become undone, if you know what I mean."

Paul nodded.

His father punched his fist into his other hand. "It's just...how do I do it?"

"No, Dad. How do we do it?"

That night in bed, Paul, who could not lull himself to sleep, came to two realizations.

Of course, Theisen has a connection to why students were becoming sick, he thought.

In the myth that Paul's dad had told, Thiassi grabbed Iduna so he could have the apple orchard for himself. The apples provided him with eternal youth.

Paul sat up in bed and gasped. Like a domino effect, everything came together for him. Theisen was Thiassi. He already knew this. The treasure was apples. He knew this, too. The apples were children and the children...Oh, I see, Paul thought. The children were the eternal youth that Theisen so needed to...To what?

Yes, Theisen was robbing them of their energy by causing them, through his...magic, to be sick and defenseless.

The other realization came to Paul just before he drifted off into a troubled sleep. He remembered seeing the picture of the driver who had smashed into his parents' car so long ago, causing his mother's death.

And that picture showed a strong resemblance to someone who Paul now feared: Mr. Theisen.

Just before the spring break, Mr. Donlevy asked Paul and Chad to see him after school. They crept back to his room without anyone knowing. They were wondering where this meeting would lead. Usually, the subject came down to one thing: Beso.

As Paul and Chad sat, facing Mr. Donlevy, Mr. Donlevy turned to them.

"This is a big year for all of us," he said. "Every year brings new things...and sometimes they aren't so good."

Paul and Chad looked at each other, understanding part of that.

"Spring break is approaching..." Mr. Donlevy went on.

Paul felt Chad squirm beside him and he knew why. He didn't need to ask Chad about these things any more, about why Mr. Tremblay wouldn't let his son dog-sit for Mr. Donlevy, about what Mr. Tremblay thought of Mr. Donlevy, about how Mr. Tremblay's drinking had gotten worse and how he was fighting more with Chad's mother.

Paul wanted to help Chad in some way but, at this time, he had too many other things to think about.

Mr. Donlevy must have noticed Chad flinching because he looked only at Paul when he said, "Can you walk Beso for me again? This time, I'd need you for two nights. This Friday and Saturday? My mother would take him for the rest of the week."

"I think it'll be okay. We won't be going anywhere. Not with Adrian..."

"How is the poor guy?" Mr. Donlevy asked.

No one acknowledged the fact that other students at Dorian Heights were feeling sick, too.

Paul swallowed. "He's...uh...He hasn't changed much in a couple weeks. He's really weak. Dad hired a nurse but..."

Mr. Donlevy and Chad waited.

Paul found it difficult to speak, wanting to be strong but failing to find the courage. "You see, Dad thought that if he hired a nurse, he'd be able to work again. But...Well, he just can't go back to work. He kinda mopes around the house, checking on my brother. The nurse tries to get him out of the house...I think she's gettin' annoyed...Anyway, things are changing...He doesn't cook as well as he used to...He doesn't even try to cook well any more."

Mr. Donlevy saw how despondent Paul was. "Listen, Paul...Paul, look at me!" Something in his voice forced Paul to look at him. "Don't give up. We're going to help you."

Paul didn't know who he meant by *we*. Or maybe he was just trying to make Paul feel better, making him believe there was an incredible entity beyond all of them. One that could save all of them.

"Yeah," Chad said, punching Paul's arm. "We'll help."

"I want to ask you something else. The both of you," Mr. Donlevy said. "If anything ever happened to me..."

"Like what?" blurted Chad.

Paul looked over. "You know what he means."

"I'd like you guys to have Beso...I watch you with him. I know he'd be happy with you." Mr. Donlevy saw that Paul was going to speak and he cut him off, anticipating the question. "My mother is getting older. Besides, she wasn't really a dog-person to begin with. She'd be fine with the two of you having Beso."

"I don't think..." Chad began.

"I don't care which of you would take him," he said. "He'd still belong to both of you. No matter whose house he's in."

Chad smiled.

"But in my house, things are..."

"I know, Paul, I know. I think we're all having a difficult time these days. I know I haven't exactly been jolly in the classroom lately but...I do have hope. I know we'll all triumph. Keep up your spirits."

Normally, everyone in the Brager household was excited about spring break. This was usually the time of year when Mr. Brager slotted some time off so he could enjoy the company of his sons, when they could go skating at Nathan Phillips Square or visit Casa Loma.

But the atmosphere in their house was morbid. Adrian stuck to his bed, reading and colouring pictures. His appetite was good and that was one reason everyone could still garner some hope. However, he rarely wanted to go anywhere else or do anything else.

Paul needed to get out of the house. In fact, he was the only one who had the inclination to change their dire situation, insisting that they all go somewhere. It was bad enough that the nurse, Darlene, was constantly in his way. Or, as she must have thought, he was in hers.

Plus she had really bad breath, as if she'd been eating cloves of garlic or something.

It angered Paul to think of her being there or why she was even needed, seeing that his dad was always around. And Paul wasn't stupid. When would his dad run out of money? He had no job and here he was, paying Garlic-Breath.

Sometimes, Paul wanted to scream.

So when he asked about walking Beso for two nights, he didn't really care what his dad would say. He'd do it even if he had to run away.

However, his dad said it was okay.

Paul was glad. Even if this meant being out of the house for a few hours, this was something. He'd wanted to do stuff with Chad over the break but Chad had his own issues. Chad's father probably wanted Chad to be confined to his house for all of the break, Paul believed. Paul started using his vivid imagination to make up fairy tales that included Chad and Mr. Tremblay. Tales like Chad being chained up in the basement. Paul got this idea from that weird Poe story Mr. Donlevy had told them once about the guy getting revenge on another guy by getting him drunk and building a brick wall around him in the basement.

So now Paul had to get creative for spring break and provide his own entertainment.

Surprisingly, Mr. Brager was even willing to drive Paul over to Mr. Donlevy's condo. Paul tried to convince him to bring along Adrian but Mr. Brager said no, he'd ask Darlene to stay while they were out.

Paul's dad hadn't done much driving lately and Paul thought it had something to do with his vision getting worse. But he soon learned it had nothing to do with that. He could still see okay, his father reassured him. He wouldn't risk his son's life, driving blind. The fact is, he didn't ever want to be stopped by police and asked to produce his licence. Then he'd have to explain why the picture on his licence was of a much younger man.

Man, Paul was thinking, how do I stop Theisen and his little tricks? He was lost in thought on the Friday night as his dad pulled up beside the condo.

"I don't know how long I'll be," Paul told his dad, thinking about one thing in particular. And it wasn't Beso.

"Take your time."

Time, Paul thought, getting out of the car. How could either of them take their time? It seemed that it was gaining on them fast.

Beso was all over him when he got the door open but Paul, anxious to return to the condo, only gave Beso short shrift in the park. Beso seemed to be aware of this as he clung to Paul in the condo more than usual, watching Paul's every move.

"Here goes," Paul said and he went into Mr. Donlevy's office, found the key, and unlocked the drawer where the journals were stashed.

As he had done last time, Paul hovered over the journals in hesitation. Wondering if he were about to do the right thing. Wondering if his nosiness would benefit him in any way.

The last time he had been in the condo, he had been curious about the journals for a selfish reason: he wanted to know if anything had been written about him. Now, he was curious for another reason: he wanted to know if there was something Mr. Donlevy knew about Theisen that Paul didn't know. He already knew Mr. Donlevy disliked Theisen but did he know what Theisen's ultimate plan was? Did he know anything he couldn't tell Paul? Paul needed to know. Anything that could save his family was worth considering. And this is why Paul felt justified as he started thumbing through the duotangs.

He quickly looked at his watch. He didn't want to keep his dad waiting. But his inquisitiveness was too great.

The most recent journal entries were at the top so it didn't take Paul long to find what Mr. Donlevy had written for the current school year. He started to read as Beso got comfortable at his feet. This is what he read:

September 8

Have a great group of students.

Very bright and very enthusiastic.

All the teachers are in good moods, their faces brown from the sun, their walks lively and optimistic.

The stunning news is that Stu Myers will not be returning. Janet is not very open about his sudden departure. She almost seems morose when the subject comes up and she refuses to volunteer any information. Maybe she doesn't know any more than the rest of us do.

Perhaps something happened in the summer because Stu was gung-ho at the end of June and was ready to see the new soccer field in September. Apparently, it was reseeded over the summer. Haven't been on duty in that area yet so I haven't seen it. The kids love it though.

The new principal is a very strange duck. Goes by the name of Mr. Theisen. Norwegian, I believe. None of us has ever heard of him before, neither as a teacher or administrator. This is odd because some of the staff like Brad and Angela have been in the system a long time. Usually at least someone knows the new principal from his past experience or reputation. From the respectable work he's done at other schools.

But no.

Could be that he's from out of town. He doesn't say much so there's no getting answers from him right now. Janet wasn't even on the interview team. In fact, she didn't know that he was replacing Stu until the last week of August. What gives?

Surely, Janet should be let in on these things by the superintendent or the trustee. This seems really unorthodox and I'd be very upset if I were Janet.

Everyone has met him by now. We already hate him.

Paul grinned when he read this part and wished he could have seen Chad's expression as he read this aloud to him.

We hate him partly because we feel he is somehow responsible for eliminating Stu. But mostly we hate him because there are no dimensions to his personality. He stalks around with this simpering grin and addresses us like a drill sergeant. He looks us up and down as if any loose fabric or muddy shoe might reveal us as inept teachers. He is no-nonsense, which is good to a point, but, only after a week, we can tell that the staff morale will be hurting.

Yet, we feel helpless against him. There is some power he holds. I know this sounds supernatural and other-worldly but there's a kind of mind control he seems to possess. We won't talk a lot about it. It's as if he knows we're talking about it.

And his handshake? The coldest thing I've ever felt. He knows it too, watching us with that big, stupid grin, waiting for our reaction.

This is extremely weird.

The kids are talking about him, too. They're as restless as the teachers.

Paul looked at his watch.

He thought about Mr. Donlevy's writing. In a way, he had travelled into Mr. Donlevy's brain and was stuck there with his thoughts. He was a little surprised at Mr. Donlevy's writing style and how strange it was that the teachers' views of Theisen matched the students' views. Maybe kids and adults aren't so different, Paul thought. Maybe adults never overcame the fears they had as kids. Maybe they had as many questions.

But most of all, Paul thought, he had already gone too far into Mr. Donlevy's personal life and it would've been weird, sitting there in class while Mr. Donlevy talked, knowing more about him than anyone else. No longer was Mr. Donlevy a teacher to him. He was more human than ever.

Paul figured he had enough time to read one more entry before his father started getting curious. He read on:

September 18

Theisen asked me in to his office for no particular reason. Chatted me up. Asked me about how the school year was going; what I thought of my students. Didn't get too personal but sniffed around a lot.

It was eerie, as if he were trying to pick up some vibe from me. I held my ground. I looked right at him and did my own share of questions. Don't think he liked this too much.

Asked where he had taught before. He mentioned a few places in Waterloo. So, he was an out-of-towner! He didn't reveal much except that he had moved to an apartment in Toronto and was looking for a house to buy.

Asked if I liked Dorian Heights. That was strange.

Talked to Joanna about it afterwards. She said that I shouldn't be so surprised. Theisen was taking turns with all of them and that they were being as secretive with him as he was being with them. If he wants to play that game, so can we, she said.

She was not surprised about Theisen's interest in my students. She and the others had also been asked about their students.

Paul stopped again and mused over this.

Even though Theisen was focused on using all of the students in his quest for immortality, he seemed mostly interested in Paul and Adrian.

Could Theisen have been singling out Paul and Adrian right from the beginning, knowing who their father was, knowing these were the boys who could supply him with the information he needed? Knowing that...?

Paul's stomach churned as he thought of Adrian.

Chapter 10: Reading Mr. Donlevy's Journals

On the Saturday, Paul followed the routine he had the day before. Except, he showed up early in the morning to take Beso out. There's no way Beso could have gone through a whole day without an accident.

There was a new concierge since Chris didn't do the morning shift but both Paul and this concierge had been forewarned of their future meeting.

As his dad waited for him, Paul went straight to the journals.

He read:

October 1

Have found two students to look after Beso the Friday of the Thanksgiving weekend.

Paul Brager and Chad Tremblay.

Both good kids who stick together and who are very good friends. They seem excited about the job.

If things work out, and if they enjoy this, I will consider them again for future dog-sitting. I really don't think Mom is into dogs. I know she likes Beso but I don't think dogs were always her thing.

Paul skipped a few entries since not everything was about Theisen and Dorian Heights. Plus, he was nervous about finding anything that might really be personal. So he had to squint sometimes as he scanned information, purposefully blocking things out.

November 20

We've got a real dilemma on our hands. Since Theisen insists on doing basement duty in the school, the students are actually avoiding use of the washrooms.

Apparently, he lurches through the halls like Boris Karloff and sneaks up on the kids, scaring them.

In some ways, I think the students are exaggerating but even the ones who never try to make trouble are raising the issue.

It's a distraction to their learning and it affects the teachers too because it's hard to carry on a lesson when, right after recess, ten kids want to use the washroom.

The students often ask me if Mr. Myers will ever return, as if I have all the answers.

They put so much trust in you. More than you think.

So I spoke to Theisen as a promise to my students. About everything. Their reluctance to come inside, etc., etc.

He just sat back and laughed. A real harsh, diabolical laugh. Did the teachers send me as their spokesperson? he asked.

I blinked at him and asked why.

No one else had approached him, he said, so he never knew this was even an issue. No students, no parents, not even another staffmember.

But can't you see the fear in their eyes? I wanted to shout in his face but I held back, aiming for professionalism. I thought of Janet. The usually effervescent Janet who now sat in her office like a helpless, caged animal.

What is it you really want from me, Mr. Donlevy? he asked and I was shocked by the nature of the question.

What is it I wanted from him? As if I deliberately wanted to be a nuisance.

And then he started drumming on the table and I took notice of that large, vulgar ring he likes to wave around.

What is it you want me to do?

Perhaps, I said, we teachers can go back on basement duty. The inappropriate behaviour has gotten less. I did not like the trembling in my voice, as if I were snivelling. I felt like I was at that first interview so long ago, surrounded by a principal, vice-principal, and two members of the parent council.

Then I mentioned how the children's behaviour was disrupting the classroom lessons. Surely this would have some kind of meaningful effect on him.

But no, oh no.

He threw his head back and laughed again. I'll give you some advice, Mr. Donlevy, he told me. You go back and talk some sense into those students and tell them to stop being so silly.

You see, this is why we don't like him. He is demeaning and condescending and won't be shaken.

I glared at him. I believe this problem will continue, I said in the calmest voice I could summon.

That's all, Mr. Donlevy, you can go now.

When I came out of the office and passed by Janet's room, she looked up at me, then quickly averted her eyes. I wondered if she had been able to hear the conversation through the wall that separated T's room from her own.

When I glanced over at Angela, she grinned at me and gave me a thumbs-up. I had not told her about why I wanted to address T but she probably figured anyone who survived a talk with him deserved praise.

Paul sat back and rubbed his eyes. Mr. Donlevy had never talked about this meeting with Mr. Theisen...They had figured Mr. Donlevy had broken his promise and had never attempted to speak to Theisen...They should have known better, thought Paul.

Paul looked at his watch.

If he could only get in one more journal entry.

With rushing thoughts in his head, Paul scooted past an unassuming, sleepy Beso, locked up the door, and made his way down to where his dad waited in the car. His dad was caught off guard.

"What's wrong? You look scared. Everything okay?"

Paul hadn't noticed how really white his dad's hair had become and, for a moment, this was the extent of his thoughts. Then he recalled what he had come for. "Beso's sick," he said quickly, out of breath.

"Oh dear. Him, too?" Mr. Brager sat forward.

"Well, not...I mean, he puked a little...On the rug...I cleaned it up." His dad waited. "I think I should wait a little longer...Just...Well until he gets settled. It's not... Like, it's not as if..."

"Do you need me to come up, Paul?"

"No...I think...I think he'll be okay...I just want to stay with him..."

"Fine, fine...Maybe it's all the excitement...His master being away and everything."

"I think so." Paul backed away from the car.

His father had been looking at the *Star* which always seemed weird to Paul, reading something he helped to produce. As if it should have been prohibited, Paul thought. Mr. Brager looked down again at the paper and, without looking up, said, "Well I've got the cell if you need me. Take your time."

And, in a flash, Paul was back in the condo. "You're sick," he told a frisky Beso who seemed rejuvenated by Paul's second coming.

And so Paul read the biggest piece of news yet and something he had not known:

December 9

I am gearing up for England and getting away from the job. Thank God for Beso who jumps around me every time I come through the door. I will certainly miss him over Christmas but Mom always treats him well. Feeds him well, that's for sure. He's always a little fatter when I return from my trips.

All the other teachers are looking forward to the break, as well. As I suspected, staff morale has gone down and, as anyone knows, when morale goes down among teachers, the kids pick up the attitude in no time. And probably take it back to their parents.

If the parents do know something strange is occurring in their children's school, they aren't letting on they know. As far as parent-teacher interviews are concerned, anyway.

There are still a number of ill students but nothing major in most cases. Parents have asked for homework to be sent home. Plus, they were able to find care-givers for the younger kids.

The parent-teacher interviews were on Friday and, out of twenty parents I spoke to, nineteen asked the usual questions: things like, What is my son's behaviour like in class? or How can my daughter pull up her marks in math? Stuff like that.

The one parent who disclosed some out-of-the-ordinary information to me was...

Paul looked at his watch. Beso had settled again. But with eyes open. Watching Paul.

...Mr. Brager. Paul's dad.
Super-nice guy. I had met him once. Early in October. Back when we both didn't know so much.
He started out talking about his heritage. How he and his family had moved when he was Paul's age from Oslo to Toronto. He was rambling at first, checking his watch often. He knew he only had fifteen minutes before I'd have to speak to the next parent.
He made a very awkward, disconnected transition from this topic to Norse mythology. I could see he was bothered, flustered about something. So I let him speak.
Did I know anything about mythology? he asked me.
I told him I was quite interested in all mythology and had quite a few books on the subject, including one on Norse mythology.

Paul stopped reading and looked over towards the bookshelf. Where *The Illustrated Book of Norse Mythology* sat. Or, at least...where it should have sat.
Paul blinked.
The book was missing.
Panicked, Paul went over and looked deeply into the gap. He felt around behind neighbouring books to see if it had been pushed back. No luck. He scanned the entire bookshelf in case Mr. Donlevy had relocated the book. Again, no luck.
Paul held his watch up to his face and cursed under his breath.

He went back, frustrated, to the journal.

Mr. Brager asked if I knew about the myth concerning Iduna's apples.

Paul's heartbeat sounded around him, in his ears.

I said, yes.

Then there was a whole section, Paul read, on Iduna, Bragi, Thiassi.

All the things Paul's dad probably didn't want Paul to know in the beginning. But now Paul did know what was happening. He felt like one of those guys in a gangster movie who would soon be wiped out because he knew too much.

And so…And so Mr. Donlevy knew, too.

And so…

Something somewhere has to happen or there's going to be a revolution. Someone has got to take the initiative. But how? What can Janet do? What can the superintendent do?

We've got no substantial evidence on Theisen.

It's not like he abused a student or anything. In the usual sense, anyway.

He'll just sit back with his smarmy grin and let us trip all over our own useless words.

Maybe I have to do something.

But not before Christmas.

I need time to think this out.

Paul closed the journal.

Mr. Donlevy needed time to *think this out.*

Then, Paul remembered his conversation with Mr. Donlevy some time recently. The one in which Mr. Donlevy had hinted about having a plan. A plan to do something about Theisen. Surely he wouldn't use violence. Not Mr. Donlevy. No way.

Paul looked over towards the bookshelf again.

Then he carefully put the journals back in the drawer, locked them up, stowed away the key, and was off.

Chapter 11: Adrian's Condition Gets Worse

Paul was having a dream but this one did not include the plunging plane. This one started with a blaring siren that resembled the screech of an angry pterodactyl and bright, blinding lights that filled his world with confusion.

There were shouts of men, giving each other instructions. One man, his face melting, taking on a blurry hue, looked right at him and said something tersely. A warning of some kind. *Get out*, maybe. *Your life's in danger.*

Paul shook himself awake. It was all too real.

Because...it was real.

He wasn't dreaming any more. Outside of his window, he saw the blinking, red lights. Somewhere, he heard the men exchanging snippets of conversation. Was the house on fire? he thought, half-asleep, a little frightened.

But he did not smell smoke.

He swung his legs around so that they dangled over the side of the bunk. "Hey Adrian."

No answer.

He threw himself onto his stomach and looked at the lower bunk.

Adrian was not there.

"Adrian! Adrian!"

Had he been kidnapped?

Paul jumped to the floor and peered frantically in all directions.

He was quite awake now and this certainly wasn't a dream.

His dad came in, looking dishevelled and very worried. "Listen, Paul, I'm going in the ambulance with Adrian." Just like that, as if Paul was supposed to understand everything that was happening.

"What? Why? I don't get it."

"He's...uh...worse...*Hospital for Sick Kids*..."

"What? What happened?"

"Can't talk now...We'll talk there...An officer will drive you...I..."

"Go then, Dad. Go then!" He felt a bit angry. He felt that he'd been left out of a crucial decision.

His dad rushed out and babbled something to someone who was just beyond the door.

"Get some clothes on," said an unrecognizable voice. "Dress warmly. It's cold."

Paul fumbled for his clothes and saw that it was about one thirty in the morning. When he came out, the officer was waiting for him. "Better lock up the house if you have a key, son. Your dad was pretty rattled. Can't blame him."

Outside, the lone police car, its light still throbbing, looked strange on the street in front of them. There looked to be a handful of curious onlookers on the sidewalk. The car seat felt cold and alien as Paul sat.

"What happened?"

"Don't know much. The ambulance got here first. They usually do. Your brother's okay. He'll be okay."

Paul wasn't stupid.

The officer hadn't put on the siren and Paul wondered why. Then again, Paul wasn't the one who needed medical aid.

"Did you...Did you see him? My brother?"

The officer nodded but didn't volunteer any other information.

"Did he look okay? Was he breathing?"

"Uh...Oh yeah, he was breathing. He needed a little help...Listen, I think it's best if you talk to your dad about this."

"What do you mean, he needed help? Did they have to give him mouth-to-mouth?"

"Well, no. Not that I saw."

"Then what did you mean...?"

"Oxygen. They were giving him oxygen. That means, your brother was still breathing..."

"He needed help. Okay, okay. I get it."

Inside the hospital, Officer Stephens (that was his name, Paul learned) offered to get Paul a drink of something but Paul felt nauseous and didn't care for anything. Stephens led him to a waiting room and told him his dad would know he was there. Then he left.

Off to fight crime, Paul thought absurdly. That was shock, he assured himself. When you start using humour to make yourself feel better.

After awhile, Mr. Brager found him and gave him a hug. Paul let himself be drawn into the embrace, knowing his dad needed it more for himself than to comfort Paul.

His dad sat beside him for a long time without speaking. He accepted a coffee from a nurse.

Finally, Paul asked if Adrian were okay.

"He...Well, I just don't get it...He talked to me a little..." Mr. Brager put his head in his hands. "This has got to stop."

Paul rubbed his back, the way his dad often tried to soothe him, but, again, it was mechanical.

"Thanks, Paul. Thanks for..."

This shouldn't be happening, Paul thought. I'm not the adult. I'm not the one who's supposed to be in control. "I didn't even hear you come in to get Adrian," he said. "How did I manage to sleep through that?"

His dad looked up. "I didn't come to get him. I was asleep, too. I woke up and he was standing there beside my bed. He looked terrified, as if he was about to fall over...He opened his mouth but nothing came out. I phoned for the ambulance immediately. Picked him up and put him on the bed. You know Adrian, Paul. This isn't him."

Paul nodded.

"This...has...got to...stop. We can't go on living this way."

Paul's jaw started to ache. He had no idea why at first, then he realized he was clenching his teeth.

The doctor, a Dr. Fletcher, approached them and said, "You're Adrian's dad?"

Mr. Brager stood up quickly. "Yes!"

"Could you come with me? I'd like to talk with you privately."

Mr. Brager's eyes registered horror. "Is he...?"

"He's okay, sir. He's okay. I just want to discuss the situation with you."

Mr. Brager moved forward and Paul moved behind him the way Beso did with him.

Fletcher looked at Paul with questioning eyes and Mr. Brager said, "It's okay. He's Adrian's brother."

Fletcher still looked unsure but proceeded to a small room where he let both of them in. There wasn't much area for them to move around. A huge sofa, looking as if it were stuffed by over-zealous workers, lined one whole wall while a matching recliner occupied one corner. A coffee table with a glass top took up the centre of the room while a box of Kleenex lay almost exactly in the middle of the glass surface.

"Have a seat," Fletcher commanded more than offered.

Paul could barely squeeze in between the sofa and the table.

"Do you need more coffee, Mr...uh?"

"Brager. No. No, I'm okay."

As soon as everyone was settled, Fletcher got started. "I won't lie to you, Mr. Brager, your son has a...very curious condition."

Mr. Brager leaned forward. "Meaning?"

Fletcher sighed heavily. "I've been in touch with your family doctor. Uh...Dr. Samuels, correct?" Paul's father nodded. "And he was...puzzled, too."

"Puzzled?" Paul asked. "You mean...You can't figure this out? Dad, that's exactly what Dr. Samuels..."

Paul's dad put up his hand as a polite hint for Paul to stop talking.

"Well what can you tell me, doctor? How can we help him?"

Dr. Fletcher sighed again. "I have to admit, I'm not quite sure."

Mr. Brager shifted on the sofa.

"You see, Mr...Brager...Adrian is fine physically."

"How can you say that? Right now, he's lying flat on his back in a hospital bed. The paramedics had to give him oxygen. I mean, he couldn't breathe. That's physical, isn't it?"

Paul looked with surprise at his father. Where was the surge of strength coming from all of a sudden? he wondered.

"Yes, yes, sir but...It's hard to explain. We've taken a blood test. It was negative. We put monitors on his heart. The ECG readings are normal. Yes, at one point, he was having difficulty breathing but...We think something else caused this. It...The thing that caused it though was...Well, not physical." Dr. Fletcher sat back, appearing helpless.

"Neurological?"

Fletcher paused before saying, "More like...emotional... Maybe even...spiritual."

"What? That sounds..." But Paul's dad stopped and looked at Paul. His voice became calm. "It sounds supernatural, doesn't it?"

Paul nodded but he knew what his dad was thinking.

"Mr...Brager...It's as if your son's energy has been sucked out of him. How long has he been like this?"

"Uh...Almost three months...But it hasn't been quite this bad."

Paul pictured Theisen as a vampire, flowing through their window and feasting on Adrian. The thought made him sick.

"Well...What can you do for him?"

"We'll continue to monitor him. We can try medication but...I have to be honest with you...it might not help." Fletcher eyed Paul. "How are you feeling?" It was the first time he had shown any kind of concern towards Paul.

"Okay. Certainly not the way he is."

"Good."

"You think it's contagious, doctor? Whatever Adrian's got?" Mr. Brager knew some things but he didn't know how Theisen's magic worked. He also knew that other students would eventually be in Adrian's condition.

"I can't say. It's all a mystery and we're doing the best we can."

"What will...?" Mr. Brager swallowed. "What will eventually happen to him?"

Fletcher shrugged. "That's a mystery, too. Listen, this could be a whole new medical condition. I mean, every disease is a mystery in the beginning. Until people get some kind of handle on it...Can you promise not to talk... Well, talk a lot about it to anyone? If the media ever got wind..."

Mr. Brager nodded.

Paul surmised that the media would soon be investigating, anyway. Numerous illnesses in a school could not go undetected.

"If anyone asks, just say he has pneumonia or something...Something everyone knows."

Maybe he was cursed by a Norse god, Paul thought. Hey, Thiassi cursed my little brother but don't fear. It's not contagious. It had gotten to a point with Paul that nothing was unbelievable.

"Can I see him? Can I see my son?"

"Sure. Why not?"

They were led into a hospital room where Adrian's body, sporting a light blue hospital gown, looked like a puppet connected to millions of strings. The gown was down to his waist so that his chest was naked and revealing countless patches hooked to wires. Paul could see that he was also hooked up to an I.V. Just in case, Fletcher told them.

Fletcher left them alone.

Adrian's eyes fluttered open and when they did, there was an audible gasp from both Paul and his father. The whites looked greyish and both eyes lacked that sheen so common to Adrian's eyes. That sheen one can see in the eyes of happy children. Adrian managed a grin.

Mr. Brager took his hand and touched his cheek which was warm.

Adrian looked over at Paul. "Hi Paul."

Paul came forward. "Hi little brother." He had never addressed Adrian this way. Something inside him collected those words and sent them out his mouth. But no one seemed surprised by them.

"We won't stay long," Mr. Brager said. "We'll let you get your rest." He couldn't take his eyes off of his son's eyes.

Adrian's hand tightened on his father's. "You won't leave me, will you, Dad? Don't leave me with...Garlic-Breath."

Paul snickered and his dad cast him a warning look.

"No, no. Garlic...Breath...doesn't even work at this hospital."

Adrian appeared slightly relieved.

"I may not be in your room, Adrian, but...I'll be in the hospital...Just outside that door."

Adrian said nothing for a long time, then his eyes started filling with tears. "Dad, I'm sorry."

"Oh Adrian, don't be sorry. It's not..."

Adrian looked at Paul whose jaw was hurting again.

"I did something wrong. Something you told us not to do."

Mr. Brager sat back. "Go on."

"Remember...Remember that time you told Paul 'n me... Well...never to see Mr...uh...Tie-son alone? Remember?"

Paul felt his heart palpitating.

"Yes, Adrian."

The tears were now streaming down Adrian's face. "Well...I did...I...I...c-c-couldn't...h-h-help it."

Mr. Brager hugged him, manoeuvring himself around the wires. "Shhh, Adrian. Don't upset yourself. I understand everything. Do you hear? Everything. And we're all going to help. All of us."

"Even me," said Paul, trying to sound cheerful.

"H-h-he...I don't know...H-h-he said stuff. I can't 'member now...And then...h-h-he did somethin' t-t-to me...I...I...n-n-never tol' you."

Paul's dad looked at him. "What did he do, Adrian?"

"H-h-he...He never t-t-touched me...He d-d-didn't even come near me...H-h-he...I don't know...I j-j-jus' got sick... You know...afterwards."

"Okay, Adrian...Shhh..."

"D-d-d'ya think he m-m-made me sick?"

"I don't know, Adrian," his father lied.

"W-w-will he hafta...you know...go to j-j-jail? 'Cause I d-d-don't...want him to..." Then, Adrian was bawling in full force.

It took Brager a long time to calm him down but, eventually, Adrian fell asleep. His dad detached himself from him and sat back again, his aging face lined with worry.

"I wanted to tell him I was sorry," Paul said, "but I never got the chance."

His father sighed heavily. "Now why would you be sorry? And try not to surprise me. I'm not as young as I used to be."

"Sorry for all the terrible things I've said to him over the years...Sorry for all the bad things I've done to him..."

"Paul..."

"But mostly...Sorry I wasn't there to protect him..."

"But you didn't even know. Did you?"

Paul shook his head vigorously. "No...If I had...Well...I guess maybe I'd be sick now, too."

Mr. Brager revolved. "Promise you won't do anything on your own, okay? We've got to work on this together... And he's stronger...We have to admit that."

Paul nodded weakly. What he really wanted to tell his dad was that he had discovered Mr. Donlevy's journals and that he had read them and knew that his dad had spoken to Mr. Donlevy about everything. That he knew Mr. Donlevy was on their side.

And so was Chad.

They could defeat Theisen all together, Paul knew. But how? There wasn't a lot of time as his father's condition was proving.

"Paul, I've made a decision to stay at the hospital all day. And probably overnight. But I won't force you. You're responsible. You've already proven that. Go back to the house, if you want. Order in pizza tonight and we'll go from there...I'll give you some money."

"I'll...Just give me time to decide."

"Sure. Of course. But don't stay, out of guilt. No one will blame you for leaving. I'm still here."

Paul stood up. "Dad."

"Yeah?"

"It's his soul, isn't it? The doctor said *energy* but it's more than that, isn't it? It's his soul. Theisen has sucked away his soul."

Mr. Brager smiled tiredly. "I think...I think you're partly right...He is sucking away Adrian's soul...but he hasn't taken all of it...Not yet."

"And that's the treasure, isn't it? Adrian's soul. The apples. No wonder that...that..."

"Careful."

"That...pig...was so interested in Adrian. In children."

His father looked away, ashamed. "I curse my past," he said. "Why did it ever happen?"

Chapter 12: The Confrontation

Paul stuck around school until about four thirty, long enough, he suspected, that everyone except Theisen would have left the office.

He hadn't had much interaction with Chad who had had a lousy spring break, he told Paul.

Oh yeah, Paul had thought, tell me about it.

When Chad asked what was bothering him, Paul said he'd let him know soon enough. Yes, yes, he assured Chad, Adrian was still alive.

As he walked nervously to the office, he thought, first Adrian had lied big-time to his dad and now he was about to do the same. However, for a good cause. He tried to remind himself of the serious nature of his action but he just couldn't get around to convincing himself. And that's bad. When you can't even convince yourself.

But what could he say? His family was deteriorating and he was angry?

He hesitated at the entrance to the office, looked in, and saw nobody was present. Theisen's door was open, as expected.

He almost lost his courage and was about to turn away when he heard, "Come in."

He went into the office and was immediately struck by how much Theisen had gotten younger in only a few days. His hair was blacker than it had ever been, his face unblemished, polished like a kewpie doll's. His frame seemed to be bursting beneath his suit. When he looked up, he appeared fake: a toy action figure staring at Paul from a shelf. Paul imagined this was what plastic surgery was like: one's face pulled so tight that the skin prevented the eyes from closing. He actually looked ridiculous, Paul thought. Maybe he wasn't so powerful.

"Uh," he said, putting down his pen. "I expected this would happen sooner or later."

"I had a wonderful spring break," Paul said, the adrenalin in his body providing him with new-found strength. "My brother's in the hospital, thanks to you."

"To me?" Theisen said with irritating surprise.

"I know who you are. I know what you want. Adrian doesn't understand but he knows you aren't good. One day, you will..." Theisen's piercing gaze stopped his words.

"Your brother was just too curious. As you are being now. That's not entirely my fault."

Paul listened to the silence around them. The halls were still.

"Did your dad ask you to come here?"

"He doesn't know I planned on coming here. He's still at the hospital."

"Well, you're a brave soul, I'll give you that. And you came alone. No witnesses around. Do you think you made a wise decision, Paul?"

"Does it matter?" Paul looked around. He saw the apples in their bowl looking as polished as Theisen's face. "I came to ask you a question."

"I can only guess."

Paul swallowed. "I want you to put me in Adrian's place."

"I see."

"Take my soul instead of his."

Theisen got up and moved around his desk. "Oh, sacrifice. How very noble. I didn't think you cared for him that much."

"More than you do!" blurted Paul.

Theisen smirked and fondled one of the apples. Paul hated that smirk. He wanted to reach across the desk and rip the stupid thing right off his face.

"So I switch you with Adrian? Is that all? But then what, Paul? You see, that's the dilemma. When I'm finished with you, I just go after Adrian again. So what's the point of your so-called heroism?"

He was worse than being physically abusive, Paul thought, slowly losing hope. He touched parts of you with his mind games.

"And when I'm done with both you and Adrian, I just go on to someone else. You see? Perhaps I go after Chad next?"

"But how...?"

"Stupid, stupid child. You think you know everything, don't you?"

"But the treasure..."

"Doesn't it all make sense now? I started with Adrian because of your father. Get it? *Started*. I have an endless treasure abounding all around me."

Paul suddenly remembered that day on the schoolyard, that day when Liz was too afraid to go in to the washroom. That day, Theisen acted so strangely, tossing snow, smiling deliciously. Because. Because he knew what the *apples* were. What the *apples* were...Something more precious than rubies.

"So doesn't your heroism now seem pointless? Why do I need you when I have a limitless supply of treasure. You can't save him, Paul, you can't save him."

Paul wondered what was the point of restraining himself now. All the secrets had been disclosed. He knew about Theisen and Theisen knew about him. Adrian and his father were already at risk. Before he knew what his body was doing, that it was taking over his brain, he lunged across the desk at Theisen. He didn't know what he had in mind, certainly not to kill him. Perhaps just to pound out all the anger and frustration he'd been holding over the past two months, pound it out against Theisen's big, smug face. It was foolish of him.

What he remembered is that he slid across the desk as if he were surfing. The telephone and fax machine banged onto the floor. Something else, a cupful of paper clips, maybe, went sailing down as well. There was a breaking sound and the soft, clinking sound of many objects scattering across the floor.

In fact, the only thing that seemed undisturbed, as if it were glued down, was the bowl and its apples.

But Paul never even reached the man. Always proud about his speed, he was embarrassed to find Theisen quicker. His hand came over Paul's in a blur of motion and Paul was face down on the desk with his hand wrenched back and his arm in pain. While Theisen's one hand grasped Paul's hand, his other pressed so hard into Paul's back that he thought his bladder would be punctured by the corner of the desk.

"Ow!" Paul shouted. "Ow! Ow!"

"I will let you go only if you promise to cool down."

Paul couldn't believe that a caretaker somewhere wasn't rushing in to intervene. Could no one hear his cries? Could no one hear the commotion?

"Ow! Ow!"

Theisen pressed even harder, using a strength he probably hadn't possessed two months ago. "Are you ready to calm yourself?"

"Ye-es. Ye-esss. Ow!"

Theisen let go and Paul moved away from the desk, his arm throbbing, his bladder bruised. He wiped tears from his eyes and felt his shoulders shudder. "You...You coulda...broke my arm."

"I could say the same about you, Paul. You did attempt to attack me. Teachers can use physical restraint when they need to protect themselves."

Paul rubbed his arm. He felt mucus bubbling in his nostrils.

Theisen handed him a box of Kleenex. "Here. You look ridiculous."

"That was against the law."

"What? Defending myself against the savagery of a student who wanted to hurt me?"

"It was against the law! I'll tell someone!"

"Who, Paul? Who can help you? Your dad? Mr. Donlevy? No one can. Why is that, Paul? Why is that? I'll tell you why. Because they can't. Or won't."

"I'll tell..."

"Go ahead and tell anyone you want. One thing I know about you is that you're honest. Tell them you lunged across my desk to try to punch me. You tried to punch your principal, Paul. Tell the world."

"I will." Paul could feel his eyes welling again. "You know, everyone in this school knows you're different. They may not know what my dad and I know but they know you're not good. No one likes you."

Theisen laughed, long and deep. "Why would I care about the silly concerns of mortals? They are there for the purpose of aiding me. Tell me, why should I care?"

"You..."

"And while you're at it, tell them why you tried to attack me. Oh I agree they dislike me. Never ever doubted it. I'm not here to be liked. But I defy you to convince them as to who I really am. Go ahead and tell them."

"Stop!" Paul screamed, putting his hands over his ears. He took more Kleenex. After he blew his nose hard, he looked at Theisen. "We'll get you. You won't get away with it."

"Okay. Sure you will." He paused before saying, "I understand you and Adrian will be..."

"Don't ever say his name again."

"Fine. I understand you'll be...planning things. Does your father really think it's that easy?" Paul glared at him. "Does he think everything will go back to normal? That... uh...your brother will be healthy again? Is he really that naïve?"

He couldn't go home just yet. He charged into a washroom. He knelt down beside a toilet and sobbed for awhile. Not because he was physically hurt. He could get over that. But because he felt useless. He hadn't accomplished anything with Theisen.

His arm began to feel better. He looked in a mirror and saw how red his face was. He massaged his arm gently, moving it around in the shoulder socket. He pulled up his shirt, went into a stall, and pulled his pants down to check his belly.

Not a bruise. Not even a red mark.

Of course.

Chapter 13: The Return of the Norse Gods

"**O**kay, I need a look-out!"

Everyone glanced at Paul and laughed. Everyone, that is, except for Chad.

"Come on, Brager, what is this *look-out* crap? Are we in kindergarten or what?" said Arif.

All of Paul's class was gathered around him in the schoolyard and they were getting some pretty unusual stares from other students. Paul had corralled them off to the side of the school. This was the best angle, Paul thought, to hide them from anyone's sudden appearance from one of the exits.

"Who do we need a look-out for?"

"Theisen. I have to get your help."

"Michael," Arif said, "you be the look-out."

"Oh come on."

"We'll fill you in later."

Everyone looked at Michael expectantly.

"Oh jeeezz..." Michael walked off.

"Just tell us if you see him comin'."

"How do you need our help?" Liz asked. "You've been really weird lately, Paul."

"Well I've got a lot to say and it's gonna sound..." He looked at Chad.

"Go ahead," said Chad. "I've seen enough already. I'll believe you."

Paul had a rapt audience. Arif couldn't have done any better.

And he started from the beginning, leaving out things, of course: his mother's death, his finding Mr. Donlevy's journals, crying after Theisen hurt him. Those things he found too personal.

Interestingly, when he had finished, no one questioned him. Perhaps because he had spoken so convincingly, almost breaking down when he talked about how ill Adrian was. Perhaps because Chad stood by his side like a bodyguard, his arms crossed defiantly, his face masking a sneer.

"So you figure he's after all of us?" asked Tony, usually the first to criticize.

"I can believe that," Liz said. "Look at all the kids who are getting sick. I passed by the office yesterday and I heard that the Board of Health is coming in. They think it's an epidemic. Parents are starting to get worried. My mom almost kept me home today."

"Do you think Mr. Donlevy knows?" said Rodrigo.

Paul was about to answer when Chad interrupted him. "Oh yeah, he knows. Maybe not as much as Paul, but he knows enough." Then Chad looked cautiously at Paul.

"Well then," Vafa said, "if we have him on our side and all of us know...Well...Can't we do something?"

"We have to play it real carefully. He's getting stronger by the day."

"And looking younger."

"Not *looking*, Elizabeth. *Getting*. He's *getting* younger."

After some silence, Arif addressed Paul. "Can't your dad do something?"

Liz glared at him. "That's kind of insensitive, isn't it?"

Arif looked humbled. "Oh...Uh, yeah...I guess he's...I guess he can't."

They all stood thinking a long time.

"Maybe Mr. Donlevy can come up with an answer," Chad said positively.

They stood a little longer, pondering their possibilities, when the bell rang.

As they made their way inside, Paul felt someone grab his elbow. He was about to turn around and give Chad a swift kick when he saw Liz, eyes sparkling. "Uh...hi," was all he could muster.

She smiled. "You were very brave, you know. Offering to give up yourself for your little brother. Just like Aslan in *The Lion, the Witch, and the Wardrobe*. Just like him."

"Uh...thanks." He felt himself blush and glanced around quickly to make sure Chad wasn't watching. He wasn't.

Once inside their room, they sat and observed a very odd-looking Mr. Donlevy observing them back. He didn't speak for a long time, allowing them to get settled. Then, he started: "I've just been talking to Mrs. Tarnapulsky." They waited, their breath drawn in. "She has allowed me to organize the next assembly." They were somewhat disappointed as they shifted in their seats. "I'd like all of you to help me. And I would especially like Mr. Theisen to be there." They all exchanged looks.

"So what's this assembly about?" asked Arif.

"It's about...Well, quite simply, it's about youth."

Again, everyone exchanged looks. It was as if Mr. Donlevy had just been out there in the schoolyard with them, listening in. One of their fellow comrades.

"In two days, March 21 will be here. And you know what that is."

"The first day of spring," said Vafa.

"Exactly. A time when the snow melts. Or is supposed to. A time for rebirth. A time for everything to start over. In a good way. I think you know what I mean."

They hadn't seen Mr. Donlevy this optimistic in three months.

Paul was feeling somewhat down, however. It didn't feel much like spring to him.

"So what do we do?" Arif, again.

"Don't worry. There's not a lot of rehearsing required. Maybe just stand up on stage together. In fact, I'd like you to be on stage with me. To show your solidarity. To say a poem together."

"Not a poem," groaned Tony.

Mr. Donlevy showed mock-hurt. "Have I taught you nothing?"

Then everyone laughed. It was a laugh a long-time coming.

Mrs. Tarnapulsky had set the assembly for ten thirty right after recess on a day that certainly didn't feel like spring. The sun had fought hard at clearing the snow but, in the end, the snow won the battle. It was still cold outside.

Six months ago, things had been different. They had all met Mr. Theisen and the atmosphere in the school had begun to take on a sinister air. Today, things were slightly different. There was a sense of the unknown floating through the school, yet there was also a sense of hope and of things about to change for the good.

Paul's class arrived like soldiers, walking rigidly, their backs straight. No one said a word. Occasionally they'd glance at each other and grin big, round grins. Partly to communicate to each other they were a team, partly to radiate confidence and instil courage in each other.

It was a big day, an important day.

The other classes filed in, too, looking just as strong and committed and together as Paul's, not realizing the reason for this assembly but feeling fresh and confident from their recent holiday. Classes seemed punctured because of absent students but the kids exchanged smiles anyway.

And everywhere, not a word. It was the first assembly Paul had ever seen in which the teachers didn't have to direct the students where to sit or how to sit. They all pushed back in perfect formation to allow room for the other students.

Mrs. Tarnapulsky had been standing over in one corner of the auditorium, looking more in control than they'd seen her since June of the past year. She peered around the room, saw Paul's class, and nodded.

Mr. Donlevy marched his class up on stage. He motioned to Paul to walk over to one corner of the stage and be near him. "I'll be giving you commentary as the assembly goes on. I want you to be within hearing distance."

Paul didn't know exactly what this meant but he knew he'd soon find out.

Mrs. Tarnapulsky walked over to the stage and looked up at Mr. Donlevy. "Mr. Theisen will be here in five minutes. He said he was very busy with office work..."

"It's extremely important that he comes."

After Mrs. T. walked away, Paul said, "Do you think he'll come for sure?"

"I don't think he'd let this go. He knows I organized it and I've been on his back for awhile now. He'll want to see what he's up against. And besides, as you know,... he'll always be curious."

Paul saw that all the staff were there, even Mrs. Franklin from the office. Had Mr. Donlevy asked her to come? Paul mused.

Soon, they heard footsteps coming down the hall outside of the auditorium. They all kept their eyes on the entrance. The footsteps stopped suddenly as if Mr. Theisen could sense the whole meaning of this assembly right through the walls. Then the footsteps started up again but at a slower pace.

Mr. Donlevy went over to the microphone which had been placed at the front of the stage. He tapped on it and said "Check, check."

Then, Mr. Theisen came through the door. He stood still and looked all around him, his face taking on an expression they'd never seen before. It was as if he were deciding what to do next.

"Come in, Mr. Theisen. Please. I was waiting for you."

He continued looking around, shaking his head. He had witnessed assemblies before. That was not it. There was an obvious...difference to this one. The entire room was charged with vitality, with an energy that pumped all of them.

His look lingered on the pre-schoolers sitting not far from where he stood. Some of the children giggled which caused some of the older ones to laugh. The sound was loud and echoing and alive in the room, a noise that they had been robbed of for far too long.

"You see," Mr. Donlevy whispered to Paul. "He is overwhelmed. He wanted eternal youth and strength and now here it is in front of him. But he can't have it all, Paul. He can't have it all. And so he is covering up his feelings well but...I believe he's a little off-guard."

Mr. Theisen's eyes fell over the students on stage and then went from individual to individual and finally to Paul.

He smiled and took the chair that had been waiting for him.

Mr. Donlevy cleared his throat. "This assembly is dedicated to the coming of spring. I see all your faces outside and your little rosy cheeks." He directed this at the pre-schoolers who peered at each other and giggled. There were a few guffaws from grade eight students.

"That's winter for ya...It can be fun but...I think we're all ready for that warm, breezy weather again."

A few of the pre-schoolers shouted in unison: "Yeah!"

Paul checked out Theisen who had a stupid, smug grin on his face. He resembled an alligator about to make a savage attack on some helpless, unsuspecting animal.

"Spring is a time for new things, isn't it? A time when flowers come out. A time when trees start to produce leaves again. A reminder of all the beautiful things that winter has made us forget." Paul saw him look at Theisen when he said this. "A time to be youthful. No matter how old we are."

There were some snickers from Mr. Donlevy's students who saw this obvious connection to Theisen.

Mr. Donlevy paused before looking at his students and nodding. They all took out folded pieces of paper from their pockets and read together:

> I once walked out on early morning,
> Saw the world's beauty there.
> The flowers had sprung up through the snow
> And cast aside the winter's blare.
>
> The earth was warm and magical,
> The trees were budding green,
> And all about me life rejoiced
> For spring's eternal scene.

The winter swept in much too fast,
Deprived us of our youth.
But don't despair since spring is here.
It ushers in the truth.

Be honest with your feelings,
Be honest with yourself.
Don't trust the liars or the thieves
Who gamble with your health.

When winter's here, do not fail
To stand up to the cold.
For spring is there within your heart
And makes us young, not old.

Mr. Donlevy had distributed this poem to them two days before the assembly and had discussed its meaning with them. He had written it himself, he told them, although he had never given it an official title. They had given it a couple of run-throughs in class but they had seemed choppy and disjointed. Today, it came out smooth and vibrant and there was a long silence in the gym before the place erupted with applause, initiated mainly by the teachers present.

Paul did not observe Mr. Theisen but he could bet he wasn't clapping.

The assembly proceeded.

There was a rap about spring by Arif and Tony and a couple of hastily-written preambles by students about the season; however, nothing compared to the resonance of the poem.

When the assembly was over and Theisen was back in the protective shell of his office, Paul was feeling slightly exuberant but he was also thinking, *Is that all you've got against Theisen, Mr. Donlevy?*

As if Mr. Donlevy knew what Paul was thinking, perhaps seeing the look of discouragement on his face, he whispered, "It's not over yet. Stick around after school. I want to introduce you to someone."

Mr. Donlevy asked Chad to stay after school, too.

The three of them were having a conversation about Beso when the classroom door pushed open and a very imposing man stepped in.

"You'll have to excuse me," he said in a booming voice. "For obvious reasons, I did not check myself in at the office."

Paul stood, open-mouthed for so long that the incredible weight in his legs forced him into a chair. "It's him," he said, his words coming out barely audible. He was not looking at Mr. Donlevy but he guessed that his teacher was smiling, enjoying this.

"What's with you?" asked Chad but he also could not take his eyes off the man.

"So you didn't have the chance to greet Theisen," said Mr. Donlevy, his voice edged with lightness.

"Oh, as you know, I've made his acquaintance before. Long ago, in fact. We never hit it off."

"It's him," Paul gushed again.

"Who's...*him?*"

Paul looked at Chad. "The man in the dream...The man in my dream."

Chad had to think back because it had been some time ago that Paul had related the dream to him. "You mean the one with the airplane?"

Paul shook his head.

"No kidding?"

"Let me introduce you two to Mr. Overland," Mr. Donlevy said.

"Overland," Paul said. "That was the name. Overland."

Overland walked over with deliberate slowness and he saw Chad cower. "Oh don't worry. I come as a friend. I come to be united with you against a common enemy."

Chad let his hand be enveloped by Overland's monstrous grasp. Yet the handshake was warm and reassuring.

Overland then approached Paul. "You must be Fredrik Brager's son..."

He knows my father? Paul thought, then erased this thought with another: *Of course he knows him, you idiot!*

Mr. Donlevy stepped forward. "It's too bad that your dad couldn't be here with us, Paul. I know he's taking care of Adrian. But, in fact, your dad arranged for Mr. Overland to be here. Your dad and I have had some phone conversations and we thought Mr. Overland's presence would be the best solution to our problem."

Overland shook Paul's hand and there was such a sense of serenity in that handshake that Paul wanted to sleep to the sound of ocean waves. "I'm sorry about what's happened to your family but I can assure you it will be over soon."

"How...?"

"No need to ask questions, Paul. Just trust me. You can thank your dad for finding me."

Paul looked at Mr. Donlevy. "How...?"

Overland interrupted. "Trust, Paul. Just trust."

"You're...," Chad started to say but Overland's eyes fell on him and he became silent.

"Everyone in this room knows who I am. You almost reached me in your dream, Paul. Almost. But I couldn't come then. There are too many other things going on in the world. Unfortunately, a lot of those things are bad. Unfortunately, I cannot fix everything."

"But..."

"I won't be here for long. You probably will never ever see me again in your lifetime. That's probably a good thing."

"Will...Will Theisen...?"

Overland shrugged. "As you know, there will always be good and bad in the world. Past, present, and future. What we need to understand is that good won't always win. Today, it will. Tomorrow, bad will win. We have to be realistic about these things. I will do my best."

"Will it go on forever?" asked Chad, gaining some courage. "Even after we're dead?"

Overland glanced at him. "Long after you're dead, yes. The spirits of the gods will go on forever. But you can always know that good will always be present. A world couldn't exist without it."

There was some silence before Mr. Donlevy said, "I must let Overland go now. He has a job to do."

"Um," Paul said and everyone looked at him. "Mr. Overland, can you hide them again? The *apples*? Can you hide them? Because...Because..."

Overland nodded. "We can certainly try but sometimes, things are even too great for the gods. But Paul, one thing you must remember: the apples will be used again for evil purposes. Evil men and women will always exist. But what I don't know is when the next time will be. It could be in your lifetime or it could be millions of years from now. It just will be."

Chapter 14: Adrian's Recovery

Paul thought he was having another dream: the shape in front of him was a blob at first, but then it transformed eerily into a body. There was a person standing not far from his bed. His father.

Paul cranked his eyelids open even further. It was a Saturday and seven o'clock a.m. How dare his father wake him up.

"Look at me, Paul."

Paul shifted. "Jeez, Dad."

"Look at me!"

Paul swung his legs over the side of the bunk bed, yawned, held his head, and looked up. In his sleepiness, he almost mustered the energy to leap upon the impostor, this man who was claiming to be his father.

Then, it all came together.

It was his father. But the father of three months ago. The younger, stronger, happier father.

Paul leapt forward like a young bird abandoning its nest for the first time. He swooped down on his dad. "Oh Dad!" he yelled and grabbed him in a firm hug. This not only meant his father was well. It meant everything else was well, too. Everything.

They did a silly little dance together and Paul felt no embarrassment whatsoever. They laughed and spilled onto Adrian's bed and laughed again.

When they finally recovered, both of them out of breath, Mr. Brager said, "The hospital phoned. Adrian..." He had tears in his eyes. Big, slippery ones. "Adrian has made a full recovery, they said."

Paul couldn't help but feel good inside.

"A nurse walked in on him at about five this morning and he was sitting up on his bed and asking when he could go home. They don't understand any of it."

"But we do," said Paul.

His dad nodded. "It gets better. Come out to the kitchen."

Paul put some socks on and followed his dad. On the kitchen table, the *Toronto Star*'s front page was laid out and on it was the heading in big, black lettering: **School Principal Dies in Fire.** Paul sat and began to read. Mr. Brager let him. Finally, Paul looked up. "No one else died."

"It appears not."

Paul felt something tight in his stomach and he suddenly felt bothered and not quite as euphoric as he had been.

"What's wrong, Paul?" His dad sat beside him.

"I'm not sure how I should feel."

"Probably the way I had. A person is dead here and we're...Well, we're celebrating in a sense. I think we have to follow our head, not our heart, on this one, Paul."

"What d'ya mean?"

"Think of Theisen as a spirit, not as a man. He is dead to us. But he'll go on. Do you see? His spirit will come back as someone else."

"But you..."

"My spirit will come back as someone else, too. In another place. In another time. But Paul, it won't be me. Let's not talk of this. Hey, we're okay. All of us!"

Paul read through the article again. "They're not sure how the fire got started."

His dad grinned. "Let's go to the hospital. Let's go get your brother!"

At the hospital, Dr. Fletcher told them he wanted to do a few more tests on Adrian just to make sure everything was okay but that he didn't foresee any complications.

After he had finished hugging his father and even Paul who didn't resist, Adrian told them how extremely bored he was.

They had to wait on Dr. Fletcher so Paul turned to his father and said, "Why not a story, Dad? Why don't you tell us a story while we're waiting?"

"Yeah!" Adrian clapped his hands.

"How about the story of Iduna and Thiassi? Only this time, tell the ending. The one you never ever told."

"Yeah!"

Their dad grinned. "Okay. Okay, I will."

So he told the story over again but this time, he included the ending.

"Thiassi, you understand, had too much pride and pride will cause damage every time. Many a man's downfall will result from pride. Thiassi was so full of himself that he believed he was indestructible and that no one could stop him. What he ignored was the power of the other gods. The gods like Odin."

"Odin? Who's that?"

"You might say the king of the gods. Of the Norse gods. It was because of Odin and these gods that Thiassi was brought down and destroyed. You see, Adrian, the story does have a good ending, doesn't it?"

Adrian nodded but looked bewildered. "How did they... destroy...Tee...Tee-assi?"

"Fire," Paul said. "They killed Thiassi with fire."

"Oh...Okay." Adrian touched his father's face, then his hair. "You look better, Daddy. You look good."

"Thanks, Adrian. And you? You look younger than ever."

"Noooo...I wanna be older. Like Paul."

Mr. Brager grinned at Paul. "Oh no you don't. Hold on to your youth, Adrian. Hold on as long as you can."